WITH THIS VOW

Windswept Bay, Book Eleven

DEBRA CLOPTON

With This Vow

Catch up with the whole Sinclair cast of Windswept Bay and the Presleys of Ransom Creek in this heartwarming, emotional story!

Cam Sinclair is ready to celebrate the birth of their baby with Lana, the love of his life. But as their special day draws near, complications arise for Lana and fear sets in. Could what is supposed to be the happy day be a repeat of Lana's tragic past for her sweet baby? It will take both families coming together to support Lana with love and laughter as the birth nears to help ease her stress.

Don't miss this special story that is sure to touch your heart.

And don't miss the first glimpse of Cam's cousin, Doctor Adam Sinclair, the hero of my upcoming new series Sinclairs of Sunset Bay coming in 2019...

CHAPTER ONE

Moonlight shimmered in the dark room as Cam Sinclair woke to find himself alone in his bed. Unease rustled through him. He immediately sat up, looking around for his wife. Where was Lana?

Getting up, he silently walked down the hallway of their ranch house. The soft light coming from the nursery made it easy to find her. He paused at the doorway. Lana sat in the cushioned rocking chair, gently rocking with her eyes closed, her dark hair cascaded over her shoulders and her body full and round with their baby, she was more beautiful than ever. A tsunami of love washed through him, holding him transfixed by its power. This amazing woman carried their baby girl in her womb and in less than six weeks, they would be parents.

For a man good at being calm and in control, he felt a bit overwhelmed about the idea of being a dad. A worthy responsibility that had settled solidly on his shoulders the moment they'd learned they were expecting. He had more respect than ever for his dad now that he understood what it meant to father a child, and to want with all of his heart to be the best father he could be.

And the best husband.

The baby, named Eva Marie, after Lana's mother, was due the week after Christmas and right now, two days before Thanksgiving, his heart was overwhelmed with gratitude for the blessings in his life.

"Hey, beautiful," he said after a moment. Her eyelids fluttered open, startled but clearing as she watched him cross the room to her. He leaned down to gently kiss her lips, catching the shadows of worry in her eyes. "Is everything okay?" He knew she was struggling to find a balance of emotions right now.

"Everything is wonderful." She cupped his cheek with her hand as her emerald eyes met his.

She had beautiful eyes. The startling color was a Presley genetic masterpiece that, though shared by her dad and all five of her brothers, was still a unique jewel tone all her own and amazing to him with the depth and clarity. And as much as she tried, he could see her struggle.

"This is going to be a busy month," she continued. "I couldn't sleep so I'm rocking Eva Marie and…" Her hand dropped to her stomach.

He knelt at her side and placed his hand over hers, felt it tremble beneath his. There was more to this. "What's really on your mind?"

She sighed. "I'm missing my mother." Her words were softly spoken but seemed to echo in the pink and white decorated room as if it were a dark hollow cavern.

His heart ached for her. "I can only imagine how much you must miss her, especially during this special time."

His own mother had been a guiding force behind his huge family of four sisters and four brothers. She still was and could hardly wait until next week when he and Lana would make an early Christmas trip home to see his family in Windswept Bay. It would be a short trip before flying back here to Texas to spend the holiday at the ranch, close to Lana's doctors. He wasn't taking any chances and the doctor had assured him that she was okay to fly there and back on the private jet owned by his brother-in-law Gage. As long as they were home three weeks out from the due date.

"I'm sure she's looking down with all her love from above."

"Yes, I know she's with me and I've thought I was at peace with having lost her. But every day this precious baby grows inside me, I ache to share this with her. I have sweet Aunt Trudy, and Sally Ann, and Gert who all stepped in to be there for me as I was growing up in Ransom Creek. They've been like my mother's angels, watching out for me. But still…" Her words trailed off. No words were needed as the deep, aching, heartfelt wish hung in the air, filling the room with emotion.

The worry that had been a low simmer in his gut from the moment they'd learned they were expecting now churned. Lana's mother died giving birth to Lana. The dangers of child birthing were ever-present in their lives considering Eva Presley had died of unexpected complications, which made it more nerve-racking.

Was it something that could be genetic? He pushed the apprehension away, not wanting to let the fear steal the joy of the moment in their lives. The doctors had told them everything was fine. Nothing looked abnormal and he held onto their words.

It was harder for Lana to let go of and he understood. She and her brothers had been brought up by her dad and his sister, Aunt Trudy. Despite the love and closeness of the family, he knew from long conversations with Lana that nothing had ever filled the hole that their mother's loss had left in all of their lives.

Cam couldn't imagine losing Lana. How had Marcus, her father, been able to handle the anguish and pain that he must have felt?

It was unbearable to Cam to even think about it.

He tried hard not to let Lana know his fear but he wouldn't rest easy until the day he brought both his wife and their baby home from the hospital.

Unable to bear it, Cam slipped one arm beneath her knees and then slid his other arm between her back and the rocking chair and scooped her into his arms. He lifted her up as she laughed, startled by his action. He stood there, holding her and his baby, and leaned his head against her forehead; her laughter died and she buried her face against his neck, clinging to him. He breathed in the fresh spring flower-scented soap that she loved. He could hold her forever.

"I love you, Lana. What you're feeling is understandable. What you need is to hold Eva Marie in your arms and you'll give her enough love for you and your mother."

She nodded against his neck. Her arms quivered and her breath stuttered against his skin as she fought back emotion. "You're right. I'm an emotional wreck right now."

"You're a beautiful mother-to-be."

They stood together for the longest time, him just holding her and then when she relaxed against him, he strode back to their bedroom and gently laid her in the bed. She was exhausted and didn't stir as he crawled in behind her. Drawing her close, he just held her and watched her sleep. His usually strong wife was vulnerable right now.

But everything was going to be all right.

It was. He'd make sure of it.

He just needed to make sure he gave her every ounce of support she needed through this last leg of the pregnancy. And this uneasy feeling in his gut that continued to linger…he'd just rack it up as nerves of a soon-to-be dad.

He was a man who was now responsible for a treasure on earth…responsibility he took with serious intent, so what he was feeling was normal. *Right?*

Maybe so, still, as he watched Lana sleeping, he couldn't shake the feeling that something wasn't right.

The morning after Cam had found her worrying in the

baby's nursery, Lana woke feeling as if she'd cried all night. Which she hadn't done. She'd actually fallen asleep in his arms and had woken as he brought her breakfast in bed. The man was amazing. She'd gotten through the surge of emotions that had driven her from bed last night and now she would get through the day. It was a good day. It was the day of her baby shower so they were driving the two hours to Ransom Creek, her hometown, where her friends and family were holding the shower for her. That thought had lifted her spirits.

Now, Lana surveyed the room of dearly loved women who had gathered in the living room of Sally Ann's Junk Shop Bed-and-Breakfast. Lana had always loved the homey, comfortable feel of this place. As a girl growing up without a mother of her own, she'd loved spending time here with her Aunt Trudy. She'd brought Lana here for all types of gatherings that her aunt and her two best friends, Sally Ann and Gert Goodnight, had at least once a week. Girls night, and they'd included Lana when she was growing up.

Her heart tugged watching the three ladies: Sally

Ann—tall and still wearing her hair bleached blonde and long, swinging in her ever-present ponytail. Aunt Trudy—plump, shorter, and a ball of energy who loved to get into everyone's business. And then Gert—tiny, matter-of-fact attitude with a heart of gold. She loved each of them and had been silently cheering them on over the last eighteen months as they'd meddled their way through helping all her brothers find love.

And that pleased her. She loved each of their wives. Beth and Cooper were perfect for each other, and Shane and Jenna were a match meant to be. Vance and Libby were adorable together, and Brice and Tara were like two stars colliding every time they looked at each other. And her dad and Karla were blissfully happy since working things out and getting married. Even her best friends, Lori and Trip, had married, and her cousin Carson and Bella. Love was rampant in Ransom Creek. The only one yet to tie the knot was big brother Drake. Oh, he was in love and had loosened up and was learning to enjoy a more adventurous life now that Maisy Love had come into his life. But they hadn't announced a wedding date yet.

Maybe soon.

She was hoping they'd come up with a wedding date soon but she knew they were holding off until she had the baby. They didn't want to schedule the wedding and take the chance of it and the baby's birth competing against each other. Plus, there was Vance and his quest to win the National Finals Rodeo in December. And Maisy had a cooking event in Vegas, too, on that same week.

Lana knew all their reasons for waiting but she was eager for them to tie the knot.

"Okay, little mama." Beth bent over and pinned a baby bootie corsage to Lana's shirt just above her heart. "It's time to get this party started."

Lana looked down at the cute pink and white concoction. "It's adorable."

"I had fun making it for you. And your brother, he's so romantic, was standing behind my chair, trying to distract me with kisses on my neck asking questions about when were we having a baby shower. Just think our little ones will grow up together."

"I'm excited about that. You already have a yard

full of "kids" but you need the human variety." Beth raised miniature goats—even had a calendar business featuring dressed-up goats.

"Tell me about it. My kids are really rambunctious right now. I was getting a calendar shoot set up two days ago and one of them head butted me when I wasn't looking. Of course, I landed in the dirt and instantly had five kids jumping up and down on my back. It scared Cooper to death and he's demanded that I stay out of the pen when he's not with me. I've agreed since with this growing belly I'm a little off balance." She patted her growing tummy. Lana and Cam's baby was due between Christmas and New Year's and theirs was due early March.

"I agree that's a good plan. I remember a few times growing up during county fair days when I was butted by a goat and ended up face down in the dirt beneath a herd of goats.

"Well, I love your little cutie-pie goats," Aunt Trudy harrumphed, "but I want a house full of nieces and nephews. You and Cooper have stepped up like Lana, but the other brothers need to get busy."

Beth laughed. "We can't wait, Aunt Trudy."

"We're holding off. For a few months anyway, as we enjoy a little us time," Jenna said, looking apologetic.

"I heard that," her aunt Sally Ann called from the kitchen. "I have the ears of an elephant where babies are concerned."

Jenna leaned toward the short hallway to the kitchen. "Don't worry, Aunt Trudy *and* Aunt Sally Ann—we're hoping to have a houseful."

"I'm ready when y'all are," Aunt Sally Ann called back and chuckled.

"Agreed," Aunt Trudy added.

Jenna was really busy getting her marketing consulting business set up. Lana completely understood her reasoning. But Lana hadn't wanted to wait. She and Cam had talked about it and after they'd married, she'd chosen to take off from teaching this year and fulfill both of their dreams of having a baby. She was happy, overjoyed, ecstatic…but deep inside there was that longing to share with her mother, and sometimes a deep sadness just overtook her as it had last night. But she wasn't going there today and pushed the longing deep into her heart and focused on the joy in the room. The joy of this time, and the knowledge that if her mother had been able to, she would have been here physically as much as she was in spirit.

Maisy jumped into the conversation and laid an arm across Aunt Trudy's shoulders. "Drake and I have to get married before we even think about babies. So you're out of luck on our end. I hope you still love me."

"Please keep loving me too." Libby grinned. "Me and Vance aren't ready, not this year anyway. I can't even imagine with our schedule."

"I will always love y'all. But you can't blame me for trying." Aunt Trudy's eyes twinkled and she swatted Maisy's hip. "I'm just getting impatient with all the excitement of getting one little baby soon, I'm wanting the whole lot of you to get busy."

A chorus of laughter and chatter ensued.

"Well," Sally Ann said as she came out from the kitchen. "If I can't have a baby from the rest of you, let's celebrate the one we are getting. Thank you very much, Lana and Beth. Let's get some delicious cake. Whoever finds the pink baby shoes inside their piece of cake gets a prize. So chew carefully," She sang the last word and everyone moved from the living room to the bright kitchen.

Lana rose from the deeply cushioned armchair and stretched her cramping back.

"Is your back hurting?" Libby asked as they walked toward the kitchen and the promise of cake. "You look a little tired. See, I can't be being tired out there trying to keep up with Vance's schedule."

"No, you don't need to be thinking about that just yet. My back is hurting some and my energy comes and goes. I can't stay in one position too long so standing up feels good."

"Maybe it'll help you. And thanks for agreeing with me. Aunt Trudy had me feeling a little guilty."

Lana chuckled. "You'll get used to people wanting to know when you're expecting. You'll learn to ignore any guilt. It's about you and Vance and when it's right for the two of you."

Since Libby had come to town and fell in love

with Vance, they'd been busy going from rodeo to rodeo ever since they'd gotten married. They were going after his dream of winning the saddle bronc championship in the National Finals Rodeo as a team effort. Lana loved that.

"So, are you excited about the big trip to Vegas for the finals?"

Libby bit her lip and looked both excited and a little worried. "I am so excited for Vance. He's on fire right now but I'm also very glad Drake and Maisy are coming to watch him compete. I'll have someone to hang around with when he's practicing. The thought of being in Las Vegas with a lot of time on my hands is a little overwhelming."

"I'm glad Drake and Maisy will be there too. I wish we could be but..." She chuckled, rubbed her baby bump and smiled at Libby. "But it's just too close to the due date. I wouldn't want to have this baby somewhere between here and Vegas."

"That would be scary. It's killing me and Vance that there is a possibility you'll have the baby and we won't be here, but we'd never want to put you at risk.

We told Drake and Maisy they didn't have to come, just in case you had Eva Marie early, but they insisted on coming. Plus, Maisy is supposed to be on that cooking show while she's in town. And they said you and Cam insisted they needed to be the family representing Vance's cheering squad. You're a really wonderful person."

Lana wrapped an arm around Libby's waist and hugged her. "I want to see him win. He has worked so hard and been so very dedicated. He deserves this. And I am so glad he has you by his side. My littlest big brother." They both smiled at her reference to Vance. "I worried about him and now he just seems so very content. It makes my heart happy."

Libby looked suddenly emotional. "I hope so, because he made all my dreams come true and I love him so much."

"And he feels the same about you."

The back door opened and seven-year-old April rushed inside, followed by her mom, Bella. She was married to Lana's cousin, Carson. She had become a really good friend.

"Aunt Lana," April called, her face lit up like the Fourth of July. "I'm so glad we got to come have a party with you for the baby. I got her a new dress. But Mom said I needed to keep it a secret until you open the presents."

"*April*," Bella cooed, a playful warning in her words. "You were supposed to keep it a secret." She shook her head and struggled not to laugh.

April's eyes widened and she clamped a hand over her mouth. "I didn't mean to. It just came out."

Lana laughed as she bent down to embrace the little darling. "That's okay. It'll still be a surprise when I pull it out of the bag. You can help me open all the gifts. How's that?"

April squealed with delight. "Yes, I'm good at opening presents."

"Yes, you are." Bella set the present on the gift table before coming over and giving Lana a hug. She whispered, "You've made her day and helped us all out by giving her something to do. She's been talking about this nonstop all the way here from our ranch."

"She's the perfect little helper."

April sparkled under the praise of the women. The child's mother had chosen her career over raising her and it had been so hard on Carson worrying about his little girl growing up without a mother. Lana felt deep empathy for April and had been so happy when Bella had come into their lives. April needed a woman in her life. April needed someone to be a mother to her.

"Aunt Lana, look at the baby boots. *They're so cute.*" April held the adorable tiny booties out to her—pale pink with silky flowers and tiny pearls for centers.

"They're beautiful and Eva Marie is going to look like a little doll wearing them. Don't you think?"

April nodded. "Can I come see her when you bring her home?"

Lana set the booties on the chair arm and patted the spot beside her on the chair. April was seven now but still small for her age. Lana wrapped her arms around her and held her close, inhaling the sweet scent of her strawberry shampoo. Over her little head, she saw everyone watching with tender looks on their faces. They all cared about this sweet little girl, too, who had needed a mother as bad as Lana did when she was growing up. Thankfully, Carson had met Bella and everyone had gotten their wish.

"You can come stay with me for a few days after Eva Marie arrives and we'll both take care of our baby. She's going to need lots of love and I think you're just the person to help with that. Plus, she's going to want to know you. She will always look up to you like a big sister. You will be very important in her life."

April turned very serious. "And she will be very important in my life."

"I'm glad, darling. Because we already know just how sweet and kind you are."

She giggled. "I'm a stinker sometimes. Daddy says so, but he's usually teasing me."

"He likes to tease. I remember when we were all growing up, your daddy and your uncles teased me all the time. But you know what? Whenever I needed them, they came running and they always took up for me."

Sometimes too much. It was her brothers always in her business that had her leaving Texas and taking a teaching job in Windswept Bay, Florida. It had been the best move of her life because while getting away from her brothers, she'd met Cam. And wouldn't you know it, the man had a ranch in Texas only two hours away from her family ranch.

"They love you."

"They love you, too, and they'll always be there for you too. So, are you excited about Thanksgiving tomorrow?"

"Yes, Mom says that my new cousins will be there. I haven't seen them since Uncle Brice married Tara. I'm excited to get to play with Jed and Paige."

"It's going to be a fun day and I know they're looking forward to coming back from their grandparent's house so they can see you."

The kids had gotten along so well at the wedding. They were at Tara's parents today but would be back tomorrow in time for the big Thanksgiving town festival that was being held.

"It's going to be a fun day," Maisy said. "And I baked some cupcakes you'll have to try. And Libby baked pies last night."

"Eating is a great part of it." Gert grinned from

where she was sorting gifts, getting them ready to pass out. "The funniest part is watching the cowboys compete against each other."

True. Everyone would be there and it looked like it was going to be a lot of fun as it would be one big potluck dinner and everyone was invited. Lana loved her little town.

"I'm just glad we got to be here for a few days," Libby said. "I can't wait to watch everyone do their thing."

"Me either," Maisy agreed. "I've never been to this one, but I love festivals and Drake said it was a blast."

"It sure is," Aunt Trudy said. "Cowboys everywhere, trying to impress their girls. You're all going to have fun tomorrow."

"Oh, it's going to be a big day." Sally Ann passed around a tray of cookies that looked like angels wearing pink halos. "Your daddy and all your uncles are frying turkeys and there'll be mountains and mountains of Thanksgiving dressing and cranberry sauce."

April's expression contorted into a look of horror at the mention of cranberry sauce. "Yuck. I'm not eating that purple stuff."

"You don't have to." Aunt Trudy reached for a cookie and took a nibble. "There will be plenty of things there you'll love. We're going to play games too. So, you and Jed and Paige will have fun with all the other kids."

That made April beam with delight. Lana was looking forward to the festival. As everyone talked about the festival April began opening the baby gifts again, Lana was able to nestle back in her chair and relax. The ache in her back that had been coming and going was coming back. A sharp pain suddenly stabbed through her lower back and she sucked in a tight breath then let it ease out as she tried to hide her discomfort.

A Braxton Hicks contraction? She tried hard to suck in short breaths without being conspicuous. It helped ease the pain. She'd known the false labor pains were predicted by her doctor to start in the last month; she decided not to mention them to anyone. Besides,

Cam was already tightly wound, though he was trying hard not to let her see it. She could tell that her serious husband, so much like her oldest brother Drake, was taking his new daddy responsibilities to the next level. She was not going to say or do anything that would make him worry more. Him catching her in a weak moment last night thinking about her sweet mother had instantly etched his brow with concern.

Her checkup was in two days and she would ask her doctor about all the pains. It would be good for her peace of mind prior to catching the jet to Windswept Bay that Gage was sending for them. She'd tell the doctor about her pains just in case they weren't Braxton Hicks or something else…her thoughts went to her mother and the constant wonder about how she felt before she went to the hospital to have Lana and ended up dead.

Not a good place to go.

Beth handed April a package and she tore into it, paper flew everywhere. Lana fought to keep her spirits up and concentrated on the little girl as she threw herself into getting to the bottom of the package. There at last she pulled out an adorable frilly pink dress and a black and white polka dot dress just as sweet.

Lana felt her throat clog as a strange mixture of happiness and melancholy swirled through her at seeing the beautiful outfits. She could see her cherub-faced baby in the outfits and her heart yanked hard. She couldn't wait to meet her baby girl. If only she lived to see her.

She blinked away the threat of tears and forced all her efforts on the happy thoughts. She would see her baby soon. That glorious day was going to be here before she blinked twice.

Soon.

Soon she would get to do what her own mother never experienced: she would get to hold her baby girl in her arms. And in doing so, maybe it would ease the ache of what she'd missed all these years. Maybe in some way she could turn back time and experience that same gift for her mother.

If only…

CHAPTER TWO

Thanksgiving Day in Ransom Creek was a big celebration right smack in the middle of Main Street. Cam was glad to be here with Lana's family, hoping it would help lift Lana's spirits. The baby shower yesterday had seemed to help her. If not, then she had fooled him because she'd returned to her dad's home with a load of baby stuff and a smile on her face. And even her eyes lit up as she spread the clothes on the bed in their room to show him. She looked better and he prayed it wasn't simply his wishful thinking fooling him.

At least she had a lot going on today with family and friends that would keep her busy and her thoughts occupied. And the weather was cooperating too, as it was a beautiful sunny day with a temperature of around sixty. A perfect fall day in Texas to help brighten her mood. They'd split up early, her heading to town with Beth and him jumping in the truck with Cooper as they'd headed out to pick up turkeys.

A lot of turkeys.

"Happy Thanksgiving," Cooper Presley called, tipping his hat to a group of ladies as he and Cam wheeled two loads of thawed turkeys past them on their way to the turkey frying area.

Cam smiled and spotted Lana helping put tablecloths on the tables. She waved and his heart clenched with love and concern for her. He and Cooper didn't take time to stop but continued down the street. All of Lana's brothers were here and helping along with her cousin Carson and good friend of the family, Trip. Cooper's brothers and friends who were helping the Presleys with the job were all set up near the center of Main Street. They'd brought in a large chuck wagon and it made a nice decoration, but it was really there because it was stocked with everything they needed to season and fry a turkey. Barriers were set up to keep the kids safe, away from the frying vats—and they were set up way away from buildings because it was a well-known fact that turkey frying had been known to get out of hand and burn things down.

"Looks like a big crowd," Cam observed, eyeing the long tables the ladies were setting up to hold the food they were expecting everyone to show up with in the next hour.

"Always is," Cooper said. "Folks around here really enjoy the community get-together."

"Me too. Though I'm not sure your sister will be doing a lot of walking around the fair."

Cooper chuckled. "You mean waddling? I'm expecting in the next couple of months Beth will be doing some waddling too. But, seriously, I'm starting to think the doc is wrong and Lana's got a couple of kids in there. Are you prepared for twins?"

Cam could honestly say he wasn't. But if it were so, he'd happily adapt. "She isn't having twins. But she does waddle—but it's a very cute waddle." He smiled, then grew serious. "I think her back is hurting her but she says it's fine. I'll admit, I'm getting nervous."

They'd reached the turkey frying area where Lana's other brothers—Shane, Vance, Brice along with Carson and Trip, who had volunteered to help them—were busy getting the large fryers heated up and ready for the turkeys.

Drake was just walking up, too, as they arrived. He carried two multi-gallon containers of oil, one on each shoulder, and he set them on the table. "Nervous about what?" His sharp, serious gaze drilled into Cam. "Is Lana okay?"

As if all the brothers were on the same radar frequency, they all turned toward Cam. Trip and Carson too. Cam hadn't meant to alarm all of them, but there was no way to hide this. Though none of them had really talked about it, Cam was pretty sure that the pregnancy had the entire sad memory of losing their mother on their mind in some form.

He rubbed his neck. "She's fine." He sighed.

"Don't get overexcited. I'm just a nervous dad-to-be…but she's having some issues. Like getting real teary-eyed and I think her back is hurting her. She just seems a little depressed at times. But she won't admit any of this to me. The quietness is worrying me…but don't get me wrong, she's happy. She sings a lot and hums and spends a lot of time in the rocking chair in Eva Marie's room. So maybe I'm overthinking this."

All the brothers were now looking at him with perplexed expressions. Like him, they were all cattlemen who understood everything there was about a cow being pregnant and giving birth. Even Cooper, and he was an expectant dad too. But Lana was the first baby they'd ever had in the family, other than Carson's daughter seven years ago, and because it was Lana, a woman and being the one their mom died giving birth too, there was a mental connection with the birth and death. Cam could see it in their eyes that they were worried too.

He looked at Cooper. "Has Beth been acting differently like that?"

"No, I mean, she's happy. She doesn't seem

worried."

"Women are hormonal, right?" Shane asked, trying to rationalize it. "Jenna said she looked like she was excited yesterday at the shower but also a little tired. And that her hormones had caused her to be teary-eyed when she opened the gifts. I think, according to Jenna, that some of that is normal."

"That could explain it," Cooper said, his brows knitting. "Maybe Beth just hasn't gotten there yet since she's a couple of months behind Lana."

"Yeah, maybe so." Cam wanted to ease the concern etching their expressions. He probably should have kept his thoughts to himself, but they were all grown men and had wide shoulders. And besides, if he had concerns that were warranted and later they found out he hadn't said anything, then they'd probably tan his hide. "But I think she has her mama on her mind."

Everyone nodded, looking solemn.

Vance looked grim. "I can only imagine what Lana might be feeling. Even I got to feel my mom's love for a couple of years before she died. It's hard for me to remember much, but I did get that small amount of time with her. Lana never got any of that, and then there was that misplaced guilt she felt, that if she hadn't been born our mom would still be alive. I can see where her emotions would be torn up right now."

"True," Brice agreed. "But, Lana is pretty level-headed so I'm thinking she'll be okay. Especially when she is holding her baby girl next month."

"Right," Shane broke in, looking around at all of them before focusing on Cam. "But you being the daddy and husband, I can see where you'd be worried about her. Maybe about the same thing happening to Lana?"

"Yeah," he said.

Drake clamped a hand on his shoulder. "Lana is strong, don't forget that. She'll pull through this. Maybe Cooper is right and the pregnancy hormones are acting up."

Cam knew his wife was strong. And level-headed and stubborn when she wanted to be. But she was also kind and tender and had a soft heart. He didn't want her heart to hurt any more than her body. "She is all of that. I'm just a nervous soon-to-be-daddy. We better get these turkeys frying or we'll have the town in an uproar come lunchtime."

Drake clamped his hand on his shoulder again, halting him. "It'll be okay. I'll be the same way when Maisy is expecting our first child. To hear everyone else say it, you and I already take life too serious and we need to loosen up. Maybe they're right and you need to relax and enjoy this moment. I'm sure if Lana feels like something is wrong, she'll let you know. She wants this baby as much as you do and she won't do anything to jeopardize my niece."

"Listen to my big brother," Brice called from where he was firing up one of the gas burners. "Everything is going to be fine."

"Thanks, fellas. I'm sure you're all right." Cam grabbed a lighter and headed toward a turkey fryer. "Let's get these turkeys frying. It's Thanksgiving, after all, and I have a lot to be thankful for." He did. That was what he was going to start focusing on. Not impending doom.

What had gotten into him anyway?

Lana stood with Cam and surveyed the dessert table. Her mouth watered just looking at the delectable temptations. "There are way too many to choose from so I'm going to go with my favorite."

Cam automatically reached for a thick, fluffy piece of coconut cream pie and held it out to her. "I had money on it that this would be your choice."

She smiled at him, and took the pie. "You know me, I just can't resist." His smile sent her insides into a swirling whirlwind as he bent his head and kissed her lips.

"I know you well," he murmured softly against her lips before pulling back and leaving her breathless. He picked up another slice of coconut cream pie and grinned. "I'm going to have a piece with you, how's that?"

"Perfect." Oh, how she loved him. "That way you won't be asking for any of mine. And if I eat really,

really fast I might be able to eat a portion of yours.”

He laughed. “Then I better eat fast.” He took a bite of his coconut concoction as they headed toward the table.

“Not fair.” Lana elbowed him, making him laugh.

“Hey, hurry up,” Vance said. “We’re heading over to the fair competitions and I’m going to burn the boots off you fellas in the roping competition.”

“In your dreams, bronco boy,” Drake drawled, giving Vance a challenging grin. “You’ve got me on the bronc busting but I’ll take you on the roping any day.”

“You’re on, brother.” Vance grinned cockily.

Cooper pushed his hat back and pinned Vance with a grin. “I plan to give you as much competition as I possibly can.”

“Me too,” Brice chimed in from the end of the table. “So none of y’all need to get too sure of yourself. I’ve been practicing. Not being on the road hauling cattle has given me more roping practice time."

"You needed it too." Shane chuckled. "And don't count me out."

Cam listened to them as he enjoyed his pie with his wife. He winked at her. "You Presley boys don't need to count me out. I'm not planning on just laying down and letting you stampede over me."

That got laughs all around. Lana leaned in and kissed him. "That's positive thinking."

He grinned. "I'm feeling pretty invincible right now."

Lana smiled up at Cam, enjoying the way he was looking at her, as if for her he'd climb mountains. Her brothers had always been competitive, and Cam and his brothers were the same way. It didn't get boring between either family.

"I'm going to love watching you, whether you win or lose," she said. "Let's eat our pie and then go see if you can whup my brothers in the roping competition." She laughed, feeling lighthearted in that moment.

Cam's eyes twinkled, and in answer, he stuck his fork into the fluffy white and yellow concoction, scooped a huge fork full up and plopped it into his mouth.

Smiling at his antics, she got a forkful of her pie and took her time devouring every scrumptious ounce of it. Despite a low ache in her back, she'd felt good emotionally today. Staying busy kept her thoughts positive and yesterday at the shower had been so nice. She'd lain awake last night, but instead of getting up, she'd remained in bed, not wanting to worry Cam any more than she already had. She'd forced herself to dwell only on the good thoughts.

Cam had grabbed a chair for her and when they reached the roping competition, there were people everywhere. He opened the chair and set it up near the line where he would stand and throw the rope. "I'll be able to hear you cheering from here," he said as she sank into the canvas seat and set her glass of tea in the drink holder on the arm. "Comfortable?"

"Very. Now go get 'em, cowboy."

He kissed her on the cheek. "I do love you, Mrs.

Sinclair.”

"And that is enough for me.”

She watched him pick up his rope and stride to the line where all the competitors were gathering.

"This is going to be exciting,” Maisy said, after giving Drake a hug at the line and coming to join Lana. "I'm so excited. I want to see my man at work.”

Lana got a kick out of watching Maisy, cooking phenomenon, really getting into soon becoming a rancher's wife. "I enjoy watching you put more fun in my brother's life. I love your spontaneous spirit.”

"I think we balance each other out very well. We are going to have a blast in Vegas. I am so sorry we will not be here for the baby's birth, unless you decide to be a couple of weeks late. But like you said, someone needs to be there for Vance and Libby, and I've got the Food Network deal. So, it's just going to be an exciting time for everyone around.”

"You on the Food Network. What an accomplishment. You've really worked hard for this opportunity. I hope you win. I'm hoping I get to watch. I'll be rooting for you to win.”

Maisy grinned. "I do *not* want to get chopped."

"You won't. You'll show them what Maisy Love is made of. Who knows—you may walk away with a show of your own."

Maisy grew serious. "You know, there was a time when I wanted that...but now, my dreams have changed. I love it here."

"Yes, but Maisy, don't give up your dreams unless you want to. Drake won't want that. My big brother always told me to go for my dreams. But my dreams were to be a teacher so that's enabled me to be wherever my heart landed, which was back here in Texas with Cam. He would tell you the same thing. Or probably has."

"He has. But, my heart is where he is. Don't get me wrong, continuing my own show is a passion of mine, but a show that would hold me to a certain area...while it's a really exciting thing to do, it's not where my heart is. There, that amazing cowboy who loves family and legacy and me, that is my heart."

Lana teared up. "I am so grateful he found you. Growing up, he and my dad held us together after my mom died. He deserves every good thing you bring to him with your love. Thank you.”

“It works both ways. Love is amazing.”

“Yes, it is. Now, love aside, our men are about to go all out to whip the socks off each other to win this title.”

“Isn’t it exciting? I love Texas men. They are so manly.”

Lana laughed. “You got that right, sister.”

Lana watched as all of her brothers’ wives gathered around and got ready to cheer on their men. There were some cowgirls competing too, and there was a time when she was in high school that Lana had been one of them.

“So, how does this work?” Maisy asked.

“Roping in Ransom Creek is a pride issue. Cowboys love to see who can rope a steer the best. You have your professional ropers, you have your working cowboy ropers, and your rancher slash ropers, and a host of other definitions. It’s expected that if you are a professional roper that you will probably do a little bit better, since you basically practice all the time.

If you are a working cowboy, which Cam and my brothers would be classified as, then your roping skills were honed in the pastures working cattle, catching strays, and bringing them back to the herd or for branding and any number of other reasons a cowboy uses his rope. Occasionally they take time to have friendly competitions like this. Despite the differences, cowboys of all types take their business serious. So that's what we are about to see."

"I'm excited."

"Me too," Libby said. "It's nice to see Vance so relaxed."

Lana nodded. "Now, Vance wears a different label. Hopefully, he's the next National Bronc Riding Champion. My little big brother has always been gifted—was a natural in everything. But he also works hard at everything he does. Being a cowboy, roping, riding, bronc riding, it didn't matter—the kid has skills and has always kept his big brothers on their toes. So, this is always good fun."

"He loves them so much. He really looks up to all of them. I know he's out there teasing them, but he respects them all so much."

Lana knew this. And as she listened to her new sisters talking about her brothers and heard the pride and love, she was so happy. Her hand went to her stomach as her baby moved.

Cam didn't get as much practice as her brothers, because he spent more time in the office than he wanted to at their ranch in Henderson, and had to leave more of their actual ranching to their hired hands. She wasn't expecting exactly that he would win, but he was going to give it his all and have fun doing it.

And they weren't the only ones competing, as they found out when they approached the area where all the roping dummies were set up in a line. The fake calf complete with fake cow skulls with horns attached— stared across the expanse at them. As if challenging everyone, or daring them, to see who put that rope around their necks the most. Of course, Cam and the Presley brothers waited in line patiently until they could all move to the line together. The town cheered as they knew the annual Presley brothers roping competition was about to start. One reason Vance was so cocky this year was because he had won last year. And he'd won off and on over the years, though his brothers had gotten a chance to wear the title some too through the years.

This competition went way back. Her dad had started it back when they were little and he'd tried to keep them busy and help them learn that competition was a good thing. She was glad to call him her dad. He'd done such an amazing job raising them. She was so glad he had finally found someone to share his life with again. She spotted him standing on the edge of the crowd with Karla. He had his arm around her waist and was smiling and pointing as he talked. Probably explaining what was about to happen and hopefully telling Karla how he'd started the tradition years ago after they'd lost their mom. He had done everything and anything he could to unify his sons and daughter while also helping them learn that healthy competition was a good thing, as long as they didn't take themselves too seriously. And they didn't really.

Lana was struck again by how content her dad looked with Karla. Lana teared up again. *Oh these hormones*… She loved her dad so much. She was so very happy to see him happy.

Cam looked at her and she got up and crossed over to him.

"Hey cowboy, good luck."

"All I need is another good luck kiss."

She smiled, reached up and cupped his face and gave him a long kiss. "Now go win this for your baby girl."

He grinned from ear to ear. "Now that's a tough one, if I lose. But win or lose, it's for you and the baby."

Down the line, there was a whole lot of kissing going on between her brothers and their loves. One thing was certain: there was no lack of enthusiastic support for this group. Lana loved seeing her brothers all so happy, and of course, being the emotional wreck that she was these days, she teared up. *Oh goodness, was she ever going to quit crying?* She was in such an emotional state right now. This was fun; this was not something to be teary-eyed about. But of course, it really was—these were happy tears because she was just so thankful.

She placed both her hands on her tummy, feeling the baby move inside her. "Root for your daddy, baby girl. He's going to win this one for you."

"Okay, fellas—get those ropes ready," Cooter, one of the older ranchers, called out.

Cam winked at her and she headed back to her seat. "You're going to be one lucky little girl, sweetie," she whispered as she took her seat, feeling her back start to hurt. "You've got an amazing daddy."

And it was so true.

CHAPTER THREE

Lana watched as all of her brothers, Cam, her cousin Carson, and Trip got their ropes swinging above their heads and when the rancher let the flag drop to start the event…well, those ropes sailed through the air like homing pigeons flying toward their target.

Lana clasped her hands together and her insides quaked as Cam's landed over both horns and he yanked it tight as the loop slid around the dummy's neck. He grinned and shot her a wink.

She waved at him in excitement as along the line

she noticed that all the ropes had hit their targets. Hooting and hollering erupted through the crowd. All the fellas spun from one to the other, grinning like greenhorns winning their first rodeos. All the women were excited, too, and shared their excitement with one another. Beth clapped. Bella and April held hands and jumped together, enjoying the moment rooting Carson on. Maisy had thrown her arms around Drake and gave him another kiss. Lori, who could probably hold her own against the cowboys given that she'd been cowgirling all her life, laughed as she tipped her Stetson at Trip. And Jenna and Libby were both in hugs with their husbands too.

Tara and her babies, Jed and Paige, jumped up and down and waved their arms for Brice. Enjoying the excitement of his new little family, he reached out and tickled Paige and then tapped the brim of Jed's cowboy hat, causing the little boy to beam up at him proudly. Brice had quickly adjusted to being a daddy and basking in the joy of his new role as a family man.

The crowd roared too. As Cooter Davis waved his hands for quiet, they all simmered down as the men pulled their ropes in and recoiled them in preparation for the next go.

Cooter watched and warned, "Get 'em ready, 'cause we're about to have the second go."

Lana waved at her dad as people slapped him on the back, and even from where she sat, she heard them telling him he'd taught his boys well. Taking the praise with a smile and some good-natured replies, he and Karla made their way to her and the rest of their group. Gert, Sally Ann, and Aunt Trudy had made their way over too.

"How are you holding up?" He gave her a hug, followed by one from Karla.

"You need to prop those feet up," Karla said, the nurse in her coming out.

"I'm fine. Really, a little tired but that's normal. I'm here for the competition. They're tough this year."

Marcus let her change the subject but she felt as if he'd ask her again later. "They are that. It'll be interesting."

Gert looked at him and stuffed her hands on her hips. "Marcus Presley, why aren't you out there competing? You taught them everything they know."

"True," said Sally Ann. "So the question is why aren't you competing?"

"That's right, get out there and show Karla what you've got," Aunt Trudy demanded, pointing to the line.

"No, this is the boys' competition."

Lana hitched a brow at him. "Not so fast. Hey Drake, Cam. I think we need another roping dummy in there. Daddy needs to compete with y'all."

Marcus held his hands up. "Who says I want to get out there and get beaten by that cowboy contention?"

"Daddy, you did teach them. You're the best cowboy I know and you know good and well you want to get out there and mix it up with them. Show Karla what you've got."

Drake and the others were grinning now as they listened.

Karla chuckled. "That's right, Marcus. I want to see what you've got. Besides, if you compete, then I get to give you a good luck kiss like I saw all them getting earlier."

Hoots went up again and all of her brothers wouldn't let it go after that and joined in on drawing him into the competition. Another roping dummy appeared and someone handed Marcus a rope. He took it, and then with a laugh and a shake of his handsome head, he strode over and joined the lineup.

Karla followed him, took him by the face and kissed him, long and hard. When she was done, she winked at him. "Now go get 'em, cowboy. Teach these boys how it's done."

Lana's hand was over her heart, she was so delighted. Her daddy looked stunned. Absolutely stunned. And it was amazing. So very amazing to know that after all he'd been through, all the years of not dating, of being alone that he had such a spunky, fun woman by his side.

To the delight of everyone, he swept his hat from his head, and wrapped an arm around Karla, tucking her close as he lowered his lips to hers…and then used his hat as a shield from everyone while he kissed her.

Her daddy had come alive. Lana inhaled a slow,

content breath as more tears welled in her eyes. She was an ongoing faucet. But at least all the tears were happy tears. Her heart was overflowing.

And by the end of the competition, to the delight of everyone, her daddy showed the fellas how to get the job done when he won the prize.

Lana watched, knowing how close they'd come to losing him over a year and a half ago when he'd had a heart attack. A lot had happened during that time, including him meeting Karla. Plus her and all of her brothers finding love.

"What are you thinking about?" Cam asked as they arrived home at their ranch later that evening.

They snuggled together on the porch swing on the back deck, looking up at the stars. "It was a wonderful Thanksgiving."

"I agree." He rested his hand on her stomach. "Eva Marie is busy tonight," he said, as the baby moved then kicked Lana in the liver.

"Oh, yes." She almost didn't tell him that her back was throbbing but then knew he had a right to know.

"She's stirred up my back. It's throbbing pretty good right now."

He sat up. "How bad?"

"Oh, it's fine. Just some minor false labor pains. The doctor said they could start about now and they have. They'll ease up. They always do."

His mouth dropped open and his eyes narrowed. "They always do? How long have you been having these?"

"Just a few days. It's fine, Cam. Really."

"Lana, you should have told me. I've been worried about you but you're not talking enough. I knew you were having some down moments but I didn't know you were hurting. We need to load up and head to the emergency room and let a doctor check you out."

"No. I have my doctor appointment tomorrow—"

Cam raked a hand down his face, expelling an exasperated breath. And then he stood, his jaw tight as he held his hand out to her. "We're going to the emergency room. I'll let someone qualified tell me you're okay."

She stared at him. The idea of going to the hospital scared her; she had to admit it to herself. "Fine." She took his hand and let him help her up.

As they were in the truck and heading toward the hospital, she stared out into the darkness as her stomach churned and her back throbbed. *This was just Braxton Hicks and nothing more.*

Surely everything was fine.

In the darkness, Cam's hand covered hers with a comforting warmth that radiated up her arm and into her heart.

"I don't want to take any risk on your health or Eva Marie's."

A sharp pain stabbed through her and she gasped.

"Lana?"

"It's okay, just an ambush pain. Thanks for being with me."

"I am and always will be. Now hold on, we're fixin' to make it to the hospital in record time."

And that was a relief. As stubborn as she'd been because of denial that anything could be wrong, she leaned her head back and closed her eyes as she cupped her stomach and took comfort in the movement of her baby.

Cam pulled up at the hospital emergency entrance and jammed his truck into park. He hopped from the truck and jogged around to open Lana's door.

"How are you?" He took her hands and helped her from the truck. His heart pounded erratically with the deepening concern for his wife.

"I'm hurting, and I'm glad you brought me in."

She was pale and when a nurse came outside, he called for a wheelchair. Unable to wait and so worried about her, he scooped her into his arms and met the nurse pushing the wheelchair. He set her in the chair and followed the nurse inside. While the nurse took Lana back to the examination room, Cam quickly moved his truck, then he filled out the paperwork, not happy that the admittance took so long when he would rather be back there with Lana. When he finally finished, he rushed down the hall to the room they'd indicated and found Lana laying on the bed that had her slightly sitting up. They already had her hooked up to a heart monitor and a blood pressure monitor. The machines were blipping and the screens were alive with data at every beat of her and the baby's hearts.

"How are you? How is she?" he asked both of them, looking from Lana to the admitting nurse.

"I'm about to administer an IV. The doctor wants to get some fluids in her because there is the possibility that she's dehydrated."

"Really?"

The nurse gave him a calming smile. "We won't know until the bloodwork comes back, which I've already drawn, but we see expectant moms in here all the time for dehydration. The doctor will be here in a few minutes."

A small sense of relief seeped into him as he took Lana's hand between both of his. "Hopefully that's all this is."

She nodded. "I'm going to think positive and trust that it is."

"I love you, Lana Sinclair." He kissed her forehead, thankful that she'd told him she was hurting.

Dehydration might be easily fixed with some bags of fluid but if she hadn't, then it could have led to what…early delivery? More pain for her and the baby? He didn't like that he felt so clueless about what to expect. He decided he needed to drill the doctor tonight and her doctor tomorrow so that he'd be more knowledgeable about his wife's pregnancy than he was about a cow or a mare delivering a colt or a calf. "I'll probably call my dad and let him know what's going on so they won't be expecting us."

"No." Lana pulled back to look at him. "Don't do that yet. Wait until we hear what this doctor and then Doctor Cramer says tomorrow. I may be fine to fly."

"I don't know. I'll be a nervous wreck worrying—"

"Wait, don't go panicking on me. I'm already feeling better. I should have told you I was hurting. If dehydration is the problem, then it's easily fixed. Please wait. I know how much everyone is hoping to see you, us. And you want to see your family too."

"I want you to be safe."

She smiled at him and cupped his cheek. "I will

be."

His heart squeezed tight and he decided he'd hold off calling his parents until after talking to the doctors. But he wasn't guaranteeing anything.

Getting on that plane was about as up in the air at this point as it could get. And until he heard the clarifications he needed, he wasn't budging on the issue.

CHAPTER FOUR

Two days later as he and Lana walked down the steps from the private jet, he had eased up on worrying some. Both doctors had confirmed that it was dehydration that had caused the back pain, and that she should be fine to fly. But he hadn't just taken their word for it; he'd questioned them endlessly about it until he'd satisfied himself that she would be fine on the plane. At least it was a private jet and an emergency landing plan had been discussed before they'd set foot inside.

Lana was feeling better, so that was good. Thanks

to the fluids but also for the great day they'd had on Thanksgiving Day. She'd enjoyed the fun day with friends and family there in Ransom Creek.

He'd wondered if maybe part of the problem was that the ranch was several hundred miles away from her family and several thousand miles away from his family in Windswept Bay. If she were closer to her friends and family in Ransom Creek, she would have had more people who loved her surrounding her during this time. Her aunt Trudy, Gert, and Sally Ann had all been there for her growing up. And then all her brothers' new wives would have been closer to her. They'd been amazing while they'd visited those couple of days.

He'd had this on his mind since the emergency room visit and he'd come to a major decision on the plane. He was going to look for a ranch near Ransom Creek, one they could live on, and he could run both ranches while having Lana closer to those she loved. The baby needed to be closer to Lana's family too. He might not be able to have his wife and daughter closer to his family because he loved Texas, but he could fix the problem of getting his girls closer to Lana's family, especially now that Cooper and Beth would soon welcome a child and Brice and Tara's children were right there along with Carson's daughter, April. He wanted Lana and Eva Marie close to them.

He loved the ranch, had loved it from the first time he'd seen it and he'd bought it as soon as he was able to after college. It was also neighbors with his brother-in-law Grant Ellington's, Cali's husband, ranch, and he watched over it for them. Because Cali's life was in Windswept Bay and because Grant spent much of his time traveling the world painting his amazing sea life murals, he wasn't at his Texas ranch often these days. So, Cam had his hands full. But his priority to make sure that his wife and family were happy was weighing on him. He'd discuss it with Lana but he was ready to make this change so that Lana and Eva Marie could be around the host of family already there and those soon to come. Because he had a feeling that all of her brothers were all about to know what he was experiencing and that the Presley family was soon to be bursting with babies.

Which would make her father and Karla happy, and also make his mother and dad happy too.

Cali was smiling as they walked off the plane. She stood beside the white Windswept Bay Resort SUV waiting for them. Tall, slender, and with her blonde hair gleaming in the Florida sunlight, she sparkled in her shimmery gray slacks and white gauzy top as she waved at them while she headed their way.

"Hey, Cali. It's great to see you," he called as she reached them.

She hugged Lana then him as she spoke. "I'm so glad you're both here. Everyone is thrilled and we have a great early Christmas celebration planned for you two. You're going to head back to Texas feeling like you had a true-blue, or true *warm* Florida Christmas. And then, by the time Christmas comes around there in Texas, when you're sitting there waiting for my little niece to come along, you'll know that you've got lots of love from our end down here for you."

"I hope y'all didn't go to a lot of trouble. We're excited to be here. And just really glad that you wanted to celebrate with us early before we go home to have Eva Marie." Cam loved his family and knew they would have done anything they could to accommodate him, Lana, and the baby.

"Really, we're so excited to be here." Lana hugged Cali again and he was glad to see the sparkle in her eyes.

"That's how we all feel. We're just excited to see you before life changes and it gets *really* busy down there in Texas." She chuckled.

He laughed. "Right. I think my honey-do-list is about to explode. I peeked at it and Lana has been steadily writing on it. Not only am I going to be a daddy, I'm going to be a handyman. There's all kind of shelves, toy boxes, and baby paraphernalia that I now have a list to put together, but again, happily."

Cali patted Lana's tummy. "He'll do whatever it takes for this baby girl. And if you need me to send Grant down there to help you, all you have to do is say the word. After all you do for us watching his ranch— he can certainly scoot down there and help you put together a baby bed or whatever it is that you need done.”

“Oh no you don’t. Grant might be able to paint like a master but when it comes to putting things together, the man is all thumbs. Just you wait till it’s your turn—you’ll see and be calling me.”

They all laughed because it was true.

Cali shook her head. “I won’t tell him that you said that.”

“He knows it. He’s admitted it to me several times.”

They loaded into the SUV. He helped Lana into the front seat, loaded their luggage into the back then jumped into the backseat and Cali headed toward the airport exit. The private jet always landed at the St. Petersburg airport, so it was nice that they didn’t have to drive in from the Tampa airport. It didn’t take long for them to reach the bridge that took them out to their small slice of paradise.

The sparkling blue water surrounded the small island he loved so much. Today, the sky was a clear sapphire blue, dotted with clouds that made shadows on the water. Sailboats and fishing boats shared the expanse of crystal-blue water and Cam felt himself relax. Island time was always a good time.

He and Lana would sleep at their small home at the beach stables they owned but first, Cali drove straight to the resort where some of the family were waiting to welcome them.

"I thought we'd have lunch here. All of your sisters get to see you two. And maybe some of your brothers. I'm not sure who all is going to show up now. But when you show up at Mom's, you'll be bombarded by the whole crew. I know that Shar isn't going to be here for lunch. She's out on an ocean release today. One of their recovered sea turtles that they didn't expect would make a full recovery and be able to ever be released back into his habitat made it, and so she's thrilled since that is always their goal and it thrills her soul to see them swimming back out to sea. Gage's too. He's with her and the team. But they'll be at Mom and Dad's tomorrow for the Christmas gathering."

"That sounds good. I'm glad we're having it tomorrow. It'll give Lana time to relax this evening."

Lana shot him a *don't baby me* look and he

hitched a brow up at her, making her smile. "He's right. This body is wearing out easy these days. I love how devoted Shar and Gage are to the sea turtles they rescue and recover at the Windswept Bay Sea Turtle Hospital," Lana said. "And then with their foundation they created and the work it does with the sea life here in Florida."

"I do too," he agreed. His sister, nicknamed Superwoman because of her lifelong devotion to protecting and caring for injured sea turtles, was amazing when it came to what she did to help take care of them. And Gage, coming into her life when he did, was the perfect partner for her. A guy with far more wealth and resources when he'd arrived here on the island. It had been a really unique love story watching them fall in love and to see how well they had been matched for their love and their lives together.

"Sounds like the two of them are doing their thing. Makes me proud," he said.

"Me too," Lana agreed and looked up at him. "Our outspoken Shar needed a certain kind of guy and Gage was that guy. Just like you were my guy."

"Aww," Cali cooed, looking in the rearview at him. "I get so tickled looking at my big brother when he's all blushy from all those sweet things you say to him, Lana. It's nice to see Mister Serious Minded Cowboy Extraordinaire turn to mush."

Cam laughed. "You cut it out. Nothing wrong with a guy getting all gushy over his woman. I'm sure Grant does the same thing over you, and if he doesn't, then he should."

Cali checked traffic as she drove into the resort drive and pulled to a halt at the front doors. "He does, don't worry. I am getting all the mushy I need."

"Good to know." Cam chuckled and climbed out of the SUV. He opened Lana's door and held her hand as she slid from the high seat. It was harder to do being eight months pregnant.

Instantly recognizing them, the bellhops greeted them with friendly welcome homes as the doors opened and Jillian and Olivia rushed outside.

"You look gorgeous," Jillian exclaimed. She was a new mama, too, and had blossomed since giving birth to his baby niece. He couldn't wait to see the little sweetheart again.

Olivia hugged him and then Lana. Her eyes danced over Lana. "Pregnancy agrees with you. You're beautiful. How are you feeling?"

"You are beautiful. Not really fair since I was all blotchy." Jillian gave a dry laugh. "But I didn't care. How are you feeling? We've been anxiously waiting to have a little girl time with you."

"Hey, what about dear older brother?" Cam scowled at his sisters—teasing, of course, and they knew it.

"You're welcome to come too," Cali said, her eyes teasing. Jillian and Olivia agreed, nodding.

"No, I don't have to come. I'm heartbroken, but I can manage. I'll let you ladies have lunch. I'm sure I can find a brother or brother-in-law roaming around here somewhere."

"Heartbroken, my foot." Cali laughed.

"I'll pick up a club sandwich at the tiki bar and go looking for any of our brothers. You gals enjoy."

He kissed Lana's cheek then gave his sisters another hug and headed through the lobby toward the courtyard exit at the back at the building. Nostalgia always hit him when he was here. He had a lot of history here at this resort. His grandparents had started it and his parents had taken it over. Now that they retired, his sisters had taken it over and they'd done a huge remodeling makeover. But they'd retained the essence of the place. Then Grant had done some of his amazing murals in various places of the resort. Including the huge one here in the lobby. The sea life on the wall seemed alive, they were so real-looking. He was still amazed that his friend and neighbor from Texas could paint so incredibly.

He could relax, knowing Lana was in good hands with his sisters. And after the last forty-eight hours, he didn't mind admitting that he was ready for a few moments to relax.

As the double doors opened, he walked into the courtyard that was beautifully landscaped, thanks to his talented sister Jillian and her vision. He strode across the courtyard and past one of the pools and then crossed the bridge over the water canal that wove through the property for the swans and paddle boats.

The resort was packed but he found himself smiling as he made his way toward the water and the beach bar, where he'd order his favorite sandwich then sit down and listen to the singer crooning beach songs and playing his guitar.

And he would relax.

"Cam. Hey, over here."

He looked around and spotted his brother Jake jogging toward him from the beach. He started smiling instantly and headed toward the beach.

"Man, it is good to see you." Jake engulfed him in a hug, practically lifting him off his feet.

"You too. What are you doing here?"

"My boat's out there docked at the pier. I had a group from the resort book a dive and I picked them up here. It's a new thing the resort is offering. It's working out for both of us. I booked it for the morning, thinking you'd be here around that time. I think Sammy Jo was coming over to join in on the lunch with Lana."

"You knew I was going to get knocked out of a lunch partner?"

Jake laughed. "I had a feeling."

Cam chuckled and started to walk toward the outdoor bar and the sandwich he'd planned to order. "You're joining me, right, or are you invited to the girls' lunch?"

"No girls' lunch for me, I'm with you. And I'm starving."

They took a seat away from the bar area, opting for a table sitting in the sand under some palm trees, closer to the guy who was singing a Jimmy Buffett song and doing a good job of it. The waitress was there almost instantly, taking their order.

"Did you finally get more help at the dive shop?"

"Man, I did. I found a new dive master right before me and Sammy Jo got married. It was a big relief knowing I had help while we were on our short honeymoon." He grinned. "I'm planning on surprising her with a longer trip in a couple of months but she had a lot going on getting her new store open, so we just squeezed everything in as best that we could. Getting married was the number one thing on our list."

"I'm just glad you invited all of us and didn't

elope."

"I couldn't do that, although I did think about it. But Sammy Jo needed a wedding with all the bells and whistles. She said she didn't, but I wanted her to have it. The sisters all came through on that."

Cam looked around the resort. "It helps that you have four sisters in the wedding business. It was a beautiful wedding."

"That was another reason not to run off to Vegas or Niagara Falls, where they, too, could have put on a nice wedding at a snap of the fingers. I didn't want my sisters to stop speaking to me. Or our mother."

"You're a smart man, Jake Sinclair."

"Sometimes. What about you?" Jake asked, "what are your plans while you're here?"

"Well, we're going to Mom's tomorrow night. We need to go home tonight and let Lana relax and rest after the trip today. I didn't call Mom or anybody and let them know, but she's been down a little bit and she had to go to the emergency room night before last. I actually had to kind of make her go because she didn't want to. But after the big Thanksgiving Day celebration in Ransom Creek, her back has been hurting and she admitted it to me at last. I took her to the emergency room doctor and he administered fluids and said she was dehydrated and that that could cause false labor pains. Her own doctor, who we saw the next day, agreed and said she should be fine and was okay to fly. I didn't want to come but she insisted.

"But I'm not completely convinced the doctors are right. Chalk it up to nervous husband and daddy. If it was up to me, I'd keep her in the house with her feet propped up and I'd wait on her all day long in order to keep her and the baby safe. But she won't hear of that. I didn't want to come here but she insisted. She won't give in to it. She may be hurting and she may be getting down at times but for the most part you would never know it looking at her. She's Lana. She's a brilliant stroke of sunlight most of the time to everyone around.

"Her brothers don't know—her dad doesn't know. All they know is that she's having regular pregnancy issues—tired of waddling, of her feet swelling—but they don't know the other stuff. And she would never tell them because she thinks in the back of their minds, they are having similar worries that she is having… I think she's down because when you lose your mom while she's giving birth to you, it has a profound effect on you. And it does a number on your mind. On your heart."

Jake had gone completely silent, stunned. his brows drawn over intense eyes.

Cam continued spilling his fears. "She's admitted to me that she used to blame herself for her mom's death. That if her mom hadn't been pregnant with her, she would still be alive and her brothers would have had a mom and her dad would still have his wife. Because of all of that, she would never tell them what's going on with her because she fears they're already thinking…what if this baby ends up growing up without a mom? What if whatever happened that caused her mother to hemorrhage like she did and die giving birth to Lana, that it could happen to her? Out of the blue, out of thin air."

"Wow. That's awful," Jake said, at last concern etched on his face.

"Tell me about it. I thought she'd come to terms with that but now, sometimes I see real pain in her eyes…it weighs heavy on her. She doesn't talk about it but sometimes it hits her. And sometimes just not having her mom here to share this with hits her. It would be hard for any woman but I think for Lana, since she never knew her mom, that it puts a hole in her heart and she's struggled a little bit…a lot, I think. She's a trooper, especially when I find her up at night in the baby's room. She's hurting inside—she won't even let me know she's hurting."

"I had no idea," Jake said. "That's, that's tough stuff to deal with…I don't even know what to say. Are you okay, man?"

Cam hadn't realized how badly he needed to talk. He gathered his thoughts as the waitress set their sandwiches in front of them. He wasn't hungry any more. As she walked away, he put his elbows on the table and cupped his hands together. "To tell you the truth, not really. I wake up in the middle of the night and sometimes she's not there. I find her in the baby's room, rocking in the rocking chair with her hands on her tummy. I know that is probably normal thing for expecting mothers. But…with Lana, it's almost as if she's doing it in case she can't do it when the baby comes." His voice broke. He looked out at the ocean and looked hard. Emotions that he had held at bay for a while ambushed him.

Jake's hand on his shoulder had him giving his brother a valiant smile. A weak smile. "Thanks. In my mind, I tell myself that we're both overreacting. It was a fluke that her mom died. A one-in-a-million chance. But deep down, I'm terrified. I'd never tell her that. But that's why we're here early, so I can get her back home. If the baby decides to come early, I need her as close as I can get her to her doctors who know her history."

"I totally understand. Everyone understands…well, to a point. None of them, like me, had any idea this was a concern. I mean, wow, I knew that her mother had died giving birth to her but my brain hadn't wrapped around the impact, the implications—the thought that it could happen to her. The fear."

"I keep thinking I need to tell Mom and Dad. But I don't want them to worry. I don't want anyone to worry. But, it's weighing on me and you showed up and well, you get it laid on your lap."

Jake was always up for adventure. The last of the brothers to get married and by most people's minds, the least likely one to confide in, but Jake was always there for all of his brothers. His head was screwed on correctly. He had wide shoulders. And Cam knew he was the right man to confide in.

Lana breathed in the sea air as they all took seats on the outside deck of the open-air restaurant that overlooked the sparkling white sand and the crystal-blue ocean. Seagulls drifted on the sea air and people enjoyed the beach and the water. Lana inhaled the salty air and felt herself relaxing. Music played from speakers across the courtyard, where the pool was packed with families. Squeals could be heard from happy kids. Here at the beachside restaurant, it was a little to the side and though there was activity surrounding it, the atmosphere was laid-back and relaxing. Lana really enjoyed this place.

"So, did you get a lot of really cute things at the baby shower?" Jillian asked. "My baby shower was so fun. There's nothing like colorful, adorable baby clothes to warm a weary mother's heart."

Olivia gave her sister a skeptical look. "Not that you were ever a weary pregnant mother. You were so thrilled to be having a baby, after having waited so long, nothing—not even swollen big toes, a huge tummy, sleepless nights, and indigestion—was going to get you down. I don't think I ever heard a discouraging word come out of your mouth, Jillian."

Jillian smiled contently. "It's true. I mean, really, I went so many years believing that I wouldn't have a baby and then my time was running out, so when Ryan came back to town and things finally worked out, nothing was going to get me down. Enough about me—this is about Lana. So, did you have fun? What did you love the most?"

Lana laughed and took a sip of the lemon water the waitress set on the table in front of her. "It was all fun. And the baby clothes are adorable. I love the colorful stuffed toys that are just the right size for the baby. I could fill the nursery up with those. And baby shoes. They are sweet." She looked around the table and then out at the ocean and felt a sense of peace come over her. "It feels so good to be here. I have missed all of you amazing women."

When she had moved to Windswept Bay to take a teaching job and to escape the smothering, overprotectiveness of her brothers, she'd met Cam's sisters through her friend Jessica. Jessica was also a teacher and had been dating Cam's brother, Levi, who was the chief of police in town. Lana always smiled, thinking of how those two were brought together through class show-and-tell. Like Jessica had welcomed her, so had all the Sinclair sisters.

And when she and Cam were married, they were her sisters, even before her brothers started giving her sisters-in-law back in Texas. For a girl who'd grown up lonely for girls her age while being brought up in a world of brothers, her cup was overflowing now.

Cali was so smart and oversaw almost everything

on the business end of the resort. Jillian was a master when it came to landscaping and all things plants. Olivia, a publicist who had left Hollywood to come home to find love and happiness, now ran the publicity and marketing end of the resort business while Shar had gone on to live her dream of saving the sea life with her husband, Gage. Shar was outspoken, unpredictable, and had a humongous heart. All of them were amazing and that wasn't even all the new sisters-in-law she'd gained as Cam's brothers had married. Her baby was going to grow up with the most wonderful family on both sides of the family tree. Looking around the table, Lana teared up.

"We've missed you too." Cali reached across to pat her arm. "Here, take this." She passed her a napkin and Lana dabbed at her eyes.

"Thanks."

"Hormones getting you?" Jillian asked, softly.

Lana nodded, finding it better not to speak for a second until she got her emotions under control or she could start bawling.

"It's okay." Olivia smiled. "You can cry all you

want. We've got your back, sister."

She laughed a teary laugh. "I have missed all of you so much. Hopefully, all of you can come down to visit after the baby is born. We have plenty of room at the ranch and I would love to have all of you guys come stay a few days. We could make a trip over to my family's ranch, too, and you could get to know my side of the family better."

"I love this idea." Cali looked around the group. "Don't you?"

"Yes," Olivia agreed. "With all three of us running the show here at the resort, it makes it hard for us all to get away at one time. But I bet we can figure something out so we can see you and our sweet niece."

Jillian nodded. "We can figure this out. We have such wonderful help who could fill in for us. That's one of the perks of owning the business together, right? We have to let go at some point and this baby is a perfect reason to give it a try."

"I agree," Cali said. "January is a little quieter so I think that would be the time to do it. Olivia, maybe you can get a plan together and on the calendar."

Olivia's smile widened. "Of course I will. Nothing will keep us away from seeing you and the baby and Cam on the ranch, in your own habitat."

Everyone chuckled and picked up their menus as they chattered about the plans they would make.

The rest of the meal was spent enjoying the sun and the breeze and one another's company. Just the thought of them coming was enough to make Lana want to jump for joy. But then, given that she was eight months pregnant, that might not be the best plan of action.

She'd been feeling better, physically and emotionally, ever since the Thanksgiving dinner in Ransom Creek. She had had a few very low moments there missing her mother and worrying that…she could die like her mother and leave her sweet baby to grow up without her.

She pushed the thought away, having had a come-to-Jesus talk with herself. She was a healthy mother-to-be and nothing indicated that she could have a repeat of the sudden, startling death of her mother.

She was blessed, she was healthy, and there was

absolutely nothing that suggested that she was going to have a problem during this pregnancy. It was just normal for a girl like her, who lost so much when she was born, to have trepidations about her pregnancy.

She was just going to have to let it go and let herself enjoy the absolute joy of this journey. The pains she'd had were normal and caused from dehydration. That was all.

She breathed in and let the salty sea breezes fill her, relax her. Looking at the Sinclair sisters and the beautiful coast line of Windswept Bay behind them, she knew coming here had been much needed.

"I needed this," she admitted. So badly. "This place is magical to me. It's just so beautiful, and the amazing sugar-sand, the cotton-candy clouds in the blue sky is perfect. It will be good to put my feet up a few days and just relax. Before Eva Marie arrives."

And it was true. Her back felt much better since the emergency room visit. She just had a few short weeks to go. She was on the countdown.

And she was so ready to love on her baby.

CHAPTER FIVE

The next evening, when they arrived at his parents' house, Cam was reminded once again how much his mother loved the holidays. Violet Sinclair loved Thanksgiving but she *loved, loved, loved* Christmas and all it represented.

As they walked into the house from the front door and walked down the short hall into the open concept living space, the tree rose twelve feet in the air of the vaulted ceiling. The ornaments were eclectic and from many, many years. It made a statement of family to Cam.

With nine children, it was a given that his mother needed a big tree to hold the accumulation he and his siblings had created for her over the years.

Lana headed into the kitchen, which was to the left of the entrance and where all of his sisters were. He watched as she hugged his mother, who immediately began mothering her. His mother was good at being a mother. Cam felt uplifted watching them together. It hit him in that moment how much he'd taken his life for granted. He'd had it all growing up. Even when his brothers Jake and Max lost their parents and his parents brought them into the family, he hadn't fully realized what he had.

He got it now.

In a bit, when he wasn't interrupting, he'd tell his mom how much he loved her. Appreciated her. And he wouldn't wait.

"You're looking like a man with a lot on his mind, son." Cam's dad came to stand beside him.

"Dad, I don't think I've told you how much you and Mom mean to me. And I'm grateful for all you've done for me over the years. You've shown me the kind of dad I want to be. And I'm hoping I can be at least half the dad you've been to me and all of your kids." He meant every word. He couldn't even fully express his feelings.

His dad's expression softened. "Son, raising all of you kids has been my greatest accomplishment and my overwhelming joy. And you're going to be an amazing dad. It changes your world, and your perspective, doesn't it?"

"It does. I just needed to tell you thank you for all you did and all you do. And I'm glad you're going to be one of my baby's grandfathers." He saw Jillian come into the room, carrying her toddler.

"I can't wait to love on another grandbaby. Speaking of babies, little April is in the house and Grandpa needs some play time."

Cam grinned watching his dad sweep in and steal April from Jillian.

"Hey sweet girl, come to your grandpa." Sam held out his arms. April practically jumped from her mother's arms to her granddaddy.

He laughed and then smiled when Lana came

toward him. He held out his arms as she walked into them and leaned her head on his shoulder. He kissed her temple. "You okay?"

"I'm fine. I love your family. And April is adorable. I'm still amazed we have two Aprils in the family."

"Me too. Thanks for coming."

"I wanted to come so badly." She looked up at the tree. "This tree is amazing."

"Yeah, it's an assortment of handmade ornaments and gifts from us to Mom. She loves ornaments and we like to buy them for her."

He smiled, gazing at the varying assortments of jingle bells and all types of reindeers and Santas wearing a variety of outfits—traditional Santa suits or swim trunks. Santas surfing, snowboarding, and building sandcastles, and diving into chimneys. There were peppermint sticks and cinnamon sticks used to create palm trees hung throughout the branches. "I've always been amazed how Mom could mix such fun ornaments with traditional Christmas ornaments like those Three Wise Men and baby Jesus in a manger."

"I love it. Show me one you made." Lana shifted to face the tree.

He slipped his arm around her shoulders and pointed at a manger made of toothpicks. "This one took me a long time."

"You made this one?" She leaned forward and studied it. "It's actually amazing."

"I don't know about amazing, but it took a lot of toothpicks and a bottle of glue."

"And a lot of time. You must have worked really hard on this. And you colored the picture of the baby and glued that in the manger."

"And I wasn't very good with a crayon." It was actually scribbles.

She smiled up at him. "How old were you?"

"Oh, you're giving me an excuse. I was about four, I think. But I can't really remember. I do remember making it though because, coloring job aside, I was very proud of this."

"You should be. I like seeing all of these. My dad tried and Aunt Trudy kept a few things but this collection just boggles my mind."

He laughed. "It would boggle anyone's mind. There is a lot of stuff crammed on this tree. The tissue paper alone that she wraps everything up in before storing it is another thing. I think that toothpick manger is nearly thirty years old."

"That's some good glue. And good storage tactics."

"Tell me about it. And I'm certain that in a few short years there will be ornaments from her grandchildren joining these."

"Violet is definitely going to need a bigger tree."

"Or maybe two," he said. "Eva Marie's will be there." The thought filled him with a joy he had never even thought about just a few short months ago.

"Maybe you can show her how to make a toothpick manger."

"I can do that." He kissed her temple and caught sight of Gage and Shar on the other side of the tree, partly hidden from view of the rest of the family.

"Your sister looks happy," Lana said, softly, having seen them too.

"Yes, she does."

"Shar said in the kitchen that Gage had a blast helping your dad and brothers decorate the exterior of the house. She said he'd bought an unbelievable amount of lights and planned to decorate theirs over the next couple of days."

"Really? I may have to go help him since I didn't get to help decorate this one."

"I think that would be good of you. Shar said Gage never had much in the way of holidays until he married her and became a part of this family."

"True. The guy is practically a billionaire, and yet, Christmas was a lonely time for him." He'd lost his mother at birth, too, but Cam didn't mention that. Gage had had a dad who buried himself in his work, and Gage had been raised by nannies until he was ten. And then he'd been raised as a little businessman, going to work with his dad every day. His brother-in-law had had a very different and lonely life. Lana had at least been raised surrounded by people who knew how to show her love and did so with abundance. He was very thankful for that.

Cam glanced back at Shar and Gage. His sister

whispered something in Gage's ear then looked at her husband with a look of love on her face that Cam found really sweet. Gage's expression was happy as he bent and whispered in her ear. Cam wondered what they were talking about and felt kind of weird watching the two of them in this private moment but his curiosity got the better of him. When Gage's hand lifted to rest on Shar's stomach, Cam's heart felt light and he smiled. Beside him, Lana gave a soft gasp and her hand went to her heart. They looked at each other and smiled.

Cam had a feeling he knew exactly what they were talking about.

"I saw that." Lana's eyes twinkled with delight.

"I have a feeling there's some big news brewing in this room tonight."

Lana leaned close. "I think so too."

"Mom is going to need that bigger tree sooner than later, I think."

"They do look like they have baby news. How exciting."

"Wonder if they'll announce it tonight?"

"I hope so. And you know what—I'm going to need a good-sized tree myself. I'm going to cherish every ornament this baby girl makes for us. And all her brothers and sisters. Though it won't be quite so full as your mom's since I'm not thinking we're going to have nine children. What do you think?"

Cam wrapped his arms around her and kissed the tip of her nose. "Darlin', I'll have as many babies as you want. I'm thinking three might be nice. We have room for a lot more than that if we decide we want more. But I'll be content with Eva Marie if that's all we're blessed with. And it depends on how you physically handle having this baby. If she is the only one we have, then I'm good with that too. Okay?"

Her expression turned pensive and he thought maybe he shouldn't have said anything. Finally, she nodded. "Okay. You always know just the right thing to say."

"I try—" He broke off as the front door opened and Max and Trent came inside, followed by a tall man Cam hadn't seen in several years.

"Who is that?" Lana asked.

"My cousin Adam. We haven't seen that much of him in the last few years. He was going to school then an internship and then he went to work in New York. I'm not sure if he might be on the West Coast now. He might have gone from New York to Los Angeles, working in some major trauma units."

They headed toward the group now gathered around his cousin. Lana thought he resembled Cam and his brothers, though his hair was lighter. When she drew closer, she saw a sense of deep sadness in the depths of his eyes…or something, as if he'd seen too much and shut down. She really wasn't sure what it was about him that made her feel this way. But she couldn't shake the feeling that something had happened to him.

"Adam," Cam's mother greeted him, embracing him as she'd done everyone who'd entered her home. "I'm so glad you got to be here tonight. When Max called and told me that you were coming to stay with him for a few days, I was so excited. It's been too long since we had the chance to spend time with you. It's been about six years, if I'm thinking correctly."

He smiled at his aunt and a dimple showed in his left cheek. "About that long, Aunt Violet. Too long. It's really good to see you. You, too, Uncle Sam," he added as Sam made it to him and greeted him with a hug.

"Good to see you. Do you still surf? I remember a lot of competitions going on out there on that water when you were around."

His dimple deepened as his grin widened, but the shadows in his eyes didn't really ease up. "I haven't had a lot of opportunity to surf in the last few years. I might have to get some of that in while I'm here. Cam, good to see you," he said after being hugged and welcomed by almost everyone in the room.

Cam smiled and Lana did too. "Adam, I'm glad we came home for Christmas. We had no idea we'd get to see you. Are you on vacation?"

Adam hesitated. "I'm taking an extended leave of absence from the trauma unit in Chicago, actually."

"Chicago. I had it really confused," Cam said.

"No, you had it right. I've only been in Chicago

about a year now. I was in Los Angeles for three years before that and New York before that."

"It's about time you took some time off and made it back here. This is my wife, Lana. We're just down for a few days before we go back home to Texas to have the baby."

"That's exciting. Congratulations. I'm glad to meet you." He took her hand briefly.

"You too, and thank you. We're excited."

Trent and Max both gave her hugs and told her they were ready to meet their niece. She was crazy about Cam's brothers.

"Is Lilly coming?" she asked Trent. Kelsey was already there and had moved to stand beside her husband, Max.

"She is. At least that was the plan before I left her working while I met up with Max and Adam. But she loses all sense of time when the end of a book is near. She's holed up in her treehouse, pounding away at the keys of her computer. I just pass a little food to her and stay out of her way." He grinned. "I'm there to keep her from starving to death."

Several laughs and agreements followed his statement.

Trent built elaborate treehouses and had one on their property that Lilly, who was a well-known romance author, used as a writer's space. Trent's treehouses were amazing and the perfect place for her to hole up and be a hermit. Lana really liked it, though. "I hope so. It will be good to see her."

"She's looking forward to seeing you too. Since Max and I were hanging out with Adam for the last few hours, she'd planned to meet us here. If she doesn't show in a few minutes, I'll go get her because she really does want to come see you two."

"Sounds good." Lana realized suddenly that quiet Trent had said more in the last few minutes than normal for him. He and Max were both quieter than the other brothers. Jake and Levi were outside on the beach playing ball with their dogs and Levi's stepson, Kevin, and like Cam, they had no trouble voicing their opinions. But Max and Trent had always been quieter and Cam had explained after serving with the SEALs, they internalized a lot.

"Adam, are you still single?" Shar asked, drawing everyone's attention.

Adam nodded and Lana got the feeling he wasn't too excited about answering. "I am. Being a trauma doctor doesn't leave you a lot of time for dating. I'm coming off of a little bit of a disastrous attempt at a relationship anyway."

"Is that why you're taking a leave of absence?"

Leave it to Shar to come right out and ask the questions they were all thinking.

"I'm not going back to Chicago. I am not sure at this point what I'm going to do. Mom and Dad are wanting me to return home to Sunset Bay and open a practice there. Or to work for the hospital there. But I'm not committing to anything at the moment. I'm just here to take a breather for a week or two. It seems I've been on the fast track from the day I graduated high school and headed to college with the goal of becoming a doctor. I was in the midst of coming to this decision when Max called out of the blue to talk. He'd had me on his mind. It hit me that this was where I needed to be for a few days, hanging out with Max and

Trent, because they and Jake and Levi had all made a major life change after leaving the military."

It wasn't hard to see or hear in his words that Adam was at a crossroads. She wondered what had happened that had brought him to that point. Something had. It was clearly etched in his eyes.

Her hand instinctively went to her stomach as the sense of urgency she'd escaped for a couple of days returned. She needed to have her sweet baby and to hold her in her arms and be done with the revolving ups and downs of worrying that somehow her pregnancy would be a repeat of her mother giving birth to her.

"Are you okay?" Cam whispered against her ear. The warmth of his breath on her skin chased the sudden chill she'd felt away.

"I'm fine. I hope he figures out his next move."

"Me too. How about you come over here and snuggle into the comfy chair next to the window and put those pretty feet of yours up?"

"I think that's a great idea."

"I'm glad you're here," Cam told Adam as he

walked with her to the chair.

"Me too." Adam studied Lana. "Are you feeling okay?"

"Yes. I just get tired and my ankles swell if I stand too long."

"Let me know if I can do anything for you," he said.

"Okay," Lana said.

"I appreciate it," Cam told him.

Lana thought she heard relief in his voice and wondered if knowing Adam was there comforted him, having a doctor in the house. She found comfort in it.

Sam stepped in. "I think the food is ready, so we're going to say the blessing and get this dinner started. We'll have our official Christmas dinner in two days, after we give Cam and Lana time to relax before they head home."

Everyone turned their attention to their dad and when he bowed his head, everyone did. He blessed the food and asked for a special blessing for Eva Marie and Lana in the coming weeks. Lana prayed right along with him.

CHAPTER SIX

The next two days were lovely. Lana relaxed on the front porch some days, watching the groups of tourists who came to the stable to rent horses and ride on the beach. She loved riding horseback on the beach and still remembered the day she and Cam rode together. He loved riding on the beach too. She was too far along to ride, so she soaked up the sun and tried to think positive. She had several of her family calling to check on her. Vance, Libby, Drake, and Maisy had left for Las Vegas. They were excited and if everything went as it was supposed to, Vance planned to win the bronc riding at the NFR and come home as the National Champion in time for all of them to be there for the birth of Eva Marie.

Oh, how she wanted him to become the champion. He'd worked so hard for it. He needed his talent, good draws on his rides, and a little luck and it would be his. It all had to come together in order for him to get the title.

It was the second day after dinner at Violet and Sam's and Lana had enough of sitting around. She knew that it helped Cam not to worry about her if she stuck close to him. But the doctors had said she was fine and sitting around was not something she enjoyed. Besides that, it was Christmas time and she needed to do some shopping. She wanted to check out Jake's wife's store Lovely You and see what new gorgeous things she'd gotten in. She wanted to go see Lilly at the treehouse because she'd heard at the party how fantastic it was decorated and she wanted to see it. The place was a unique experience, to say the least. She'd have to go by maybe later that night with Cam so they could see the lights that Trent had decorated the exterior with—it, too, was supposed to be spectacular.

She picked up her keys and walked across the yard to where Cam was riding the newest horses that Kelsey had brought in for the stables. He liked to make sure himself that they were safe rides for the tourists before he gave them the okay. He was not happy that she was going on an excursion without him but the cowboy had learned early that she had a mind of her own and she liked to use it.

He was strong-willed but so was she. She'd had to be, growing up with five older brothers and a protective dad. Those six men in her life would have completely ruled her if she hadn't learned early that she had an opinion and that she liked it. Thankfully, Cam understood her and she knew he wanted to protest, his expression told her exactly what his thoughts were because he wasn't trying to hide it from her. Still, he hugged her, told her to be careful, and to call if she needed anything. And to have a good time. He'd managed the last without choking and she'd kissed his cheek. She loved him dearly.

She met her best friend, Jessica, in town. Ever

since Jessica and Cam's brother Levi had gotten together, her friend had blossomed. Levi loved her little boy and so did all the Sinclair clan. She expected that Jessica would have already given Kevin a baby sister or brother. She'd expect that at least some of his siblings would have started families in the nearly two years since she and Cam had married. But so far, Jillian and Ryan were the only ones to give Violet and Sam a grandchild. Of course, there's nothing wrong with people getting married and waiting to have babies. She smiled at that thought because just like she'd expressed to Libby at the baby shower, Lana couldn't count high enough how many times she'd been asked when she and Cam were starting a family. She was sure all of the others were asked the same question. And, of course, the answer was: *when they were ready*. Lana refused to ask any of them that question and would just wait until it happened and they announced it. In the meantime, between when she and Cam had married and gotten pregnant, they'd thoroughly enjoyed the time it was just the two of them. It had been a much-needed time of getting to know each other as husband and wife, of learning to adapt to sharing space with each other, of forming a bond between them that she cherished. Their bond would make their family unit stronger.

Still, with so many brothers and sisters, it seemed someone would have been sharing the baby spotlight with them. She thought of Shar and Gage. She was almost certain they were bursting with baby news. She just hoped they shared it before she and Cam headed back home.

Maybe it was simply that she was so excited and wanting her baby so much that she thought everyone would want their families to expand also.

Excitement hummed through her despite how she kept worrying and stressing and having her dark moments of fear that she might die and never get to hold her baby. Never get to snuggle her sweet little body in her arms and watch her smile as she slept…Lana had prayed that God would help her deal with what she was struggling with and her heart went out to all those babies who'd lost a parent like she had. And to all the parents who'd lost babies. Both were unimaginable tragedies. Unspeakable pain…

Her mind reeling, her fingers tightened on the steering wheel as she pulled into an empty parking space down the street from Sammy Jo's shop and near the coffee shop. Jessica had said she'd be grabbing them a specialty coffee and she'd meet her outside. Lana's heart thundered and her hands trembled and her mind raced with where her thoughts had gone.

Getting out and about was a good idea. She needed to move, to get out in the December balmy air of Windswept Bay. She carefully eased out of the truck seat to the pavement, her big stomach making it a little harder to do than normal. Closing the door, she glanced down toward Lovely You, Sammy Jo's custom designed clothing and gift shop.

"Lana."

Hearing Jessica's voice, she turned to see her friend coming toward her. She carried two paper cups and wore a huge smile. "Hi. Please tell me that's what I think it is."

Jessica nodded and handed her a cup. *"Decaf* pumpkin spice café latte. Your favorite."

Lana sighed. "I love you. I truly, truly do." Her senses filled with the fragrant cinnamon and pumpkin scent. Sighing again she closed her eyes and let herself enjoy it. "Thank you for the decaf. I am not drinking regular coffee right now, so the decaf is fantastic."

"And let me tell you, that new coffee shop makes a delicious concoction. You may hate me because you'll start having cravings. I do and I'm not pregnant." She laughed.

Lana took a sip, and nearly gasped with happiness. "Oh my goodness. I'm already craving my next cup. And are you sure you're not expecting?"

Jessica winked. "We better head toward Sammy Jo's or she's going to think we got lost."

Lana's eyes narrowed as she watched her buddy walking away. "Wait, you *are* expecting." She hurried as best that she could then slowed. "Don't you tease me."

Jessica spun and a bright smile split across her face. "We are, and we're trying to wait until at least the third month to tell everyone. But I told Levi I couldn't not tell you while you were home. So he agreed to let you and Cam in on the secret. I couldn't help teasing you."

Lana teared up. "Oh Jess, I am so happy for you." She threw her arms around her friend and hugged her so tightly. "I know Kevin is thrilled too."

"Oh, no, we haven't told him yet. He would tell everyone and then drive us crazy for the entire nine months with questions. We figure six months of nonstop excitement will be enough."

"I get that." She chuckled. Anyone who knew Kevin would get this logic. He would be bouncing off the walls with excitement. "But you're not telling anyone else? No one?"

"Nope. Just you and Cam. After your Eva Marie is born, we'll tell. And you can't tell anyone. Levi is going to tell Cam. He might even be out there at the stables doing it now."

"Okay, I won't tell, but it's going to really be hard to keep such a fantastic secret."

"But you can do it, for me."

"Yes, I can do it for you."

"I knew I could share this with you and trust you

at the same time. I want to share it with everyone but we just think it's better to wait. Now, let's go shopping. Sammy Jo has some new adorable baby clothes in. And she always has the most fantastic blouses and skirts. Then there are some really cute shops that have opened since you were here last. Oh, Lilly was going to come shopping with us, since she's just finished her book deadline but she got this new book idea and decided she'd get that on paper and wait for us at the treehouse. She's prepared lunch for us."

Lana blinked. "Lilly prepared lunch for us?"

"I know, hard to believe from the gal who lives on peanut butter sandwiches and coffee when she's immersed in writing a book. But since she married Trent, she's been trying hard to get more balance in her life. She struggles with it some but has a much more normal lifestyle now and isn't a hermit all of the time. She even started dabbling in cooking. She watches the Food Network and is excited to watch Maisy next week. She couldn't believe it when she learned one of your brothers was marrying one of the contestants. She can't wait until next week. Everyone who can get off is going to meet at her place and watch it together. That competition with Maisy and all the other competitors from the country is filmed live. Lilly is a fan so she'll enjoy visiting with you about that. I'm surprised she didn't pull you to the side at dinner the other night but I think she wanted to give you time with the family."

"That was sweet of her. I'm looking forward to watching it too."

They entered Sammy Jo's store and it was as lovely as the name. The colors of fabrics that she used for her creations were like artwork.

At the tinkle of the door chime, Sammy Jo spun from where she was adjusting a blouse on a hanger. She came toward them in a rush. "You made it. I'm so excited. Come back here—I have a beautiful outfit for Eva Marie."

"You didn't have to do that. But you know I can't resist because your things are so wonderful. I can't wait to see it."

Sammy Jo led the way to the back counter. She picked up a beautifully wrapped box and handed it to Lana. Lana set her coffee on the counter, away from anything that it could turn over on and destroy. The last thing she wanted to do was spill pumpkin spice café latte on anything in the store. She was taking no chances. Jessica did the same then stood eagerly as Lana lifted the lid from the box and found a beautiful dress inside. The material was a unique blend of warm red—it wasn't orange but it wasn't blood red; it was like a sunset fading from both colors and through it was a mingled shot of blush pink. She looked at Sammy Jo. "It's perfect."

"Amazing," Jessica added in awe.

Sammy Jo was a kind, sweet-spirited person and she looked extremely pleased. "When I created those colors, I had you in mind. I'm so thrilled and excited because I had just found out that the baby was going to be a little girl. So, I worked with the colors and I call it Mother and Daughter. You're the dark tone; it represents your heart and your love. And the pale pink or blush is your sweet baby. It represents how your lives will forever be mingled together and how she will always be wrapped in your love. Always."

Lana's heart cracked. All that she had been feeling

and experiencing swelled within her. She laid her hand on the cloth, and wondered whether Sammy Jo had any idea how deeply she'd just touched her.

She looked from the cloth to Sammy Jo. "It's truly lovely, like the name. It is just breathtakin—" her words broke off as a sharp pain ripped through her. Crying out in agony, Lana doubled over as her knees melted beneath her. She fell to her knees then crumpled onto the floor.

"Lana," she heard Sammy Jo scream as she dropped down beside her. "*Jessica*, she's in pain."

"I'm calling 911," Jessica said.

They sounded as if they were miles away as the room spun and Lana closed her eyes, wrapped her hands around her stomach and held onto her precious baby.

Cam had just been learning about Levi and Jessica expecting a baby when Jessica called. His heart nearly stopped beating when she told him they were rushing Lana to the hospital. He and Levi had ran to Levi's police car and his brother had turned on the emergency lights and cleared the path through the streets of Windswept Bay, scattering cars as he got Cam to the hospital in record time.

Cam had thrown himself from the car before it was completely stopped and bolted into the emergency room. "Where is my wife, Lana Sinclair?" he'd demanded and thought he was going to go crazy before they took him down the hall to where she was. As the nurse took him down the hallway Jessica and Sammy Jo rushed to him from the waiting area. Both of them looked terrified as they reached out and touched his arm in comfort as he followed the nurse.

"Let us know what the doctor says," Jessica called from behind him.

His heart had buckled at seeing the fear written on their faces. "I will," he called back, his words gruff. When the nurse took him through double doors and then showed him into a room he spotted Lana on the bed hooked up to all kinds of monitors. She was so pale.

"Lana," he whispered as he crossed to her and

gently took her hand.

"Cam," she cried, as she opened her eyes. "Oh Cam. Tell me it's going to be alright."

"It will be," he said, pushing her hair from her face and held her hand as his heart spiraled with fear as he realized he had no control over the outcome of his wife and his child's wellbeing.

Later, he was still holding her hand as the doctor examined her. Her hand was chilled to the bone. Her eyes were closed and she was pale as the white pillowcase nestling her dark hair. He'd never been so terrified in all of his life.

"It's going to be okay, Lana." He never felt so helpless.

When the doctor finished the exam, he came to stand on the other side of the bed across from Cam. "The baby is fine at the moment. We're monitoring you and the baby," he said, to Lana. "There was some bleeding but it's under control at the moment. I'll know more as soon as we get the bloodwork back. Meanwhile, we're going to admit you. You're right on the cusp of thirty-five weeks. Ideally, we'd like the baby to make it to forty weeks and be full term but we will probably not make it to that goal. Thirty-seven is far better for the baby than now, so we are going to do everything in our power to get you and the baby safe through the next two weeks. And that may mean you staying here with us for the duration. Again, I'll know more as soon as I have the test results. But, be prepared that most likely, you'll stay here with us so we'll be able to give you the care you need, and then we'll deliver a healthy baby girl."

"We'll do whatever it takes, Doctor. Thank you," Cam said and shook the doctors hand before he left.

Lana looked at him. "I'm scared, Cam."

"I'm scared too, darlin'. But all we can do is wait and pray. The good thing is that you can rest here in this bed until we find out the results and then they'll move you to a better room with a more comfortable bed. And you'll be monitored and the delivery team will be right here, ready if we need them."

"You're right. We'll do whatever needs to be done. I was spotting and it horrified me." Tears pooled in her eyes and she clamped them shut as the tears rolled down her cheeks.

Cam wiped them away with his free hand while continuing to hold her hand with his other. A fierce need to protect her gripped him. His instinct was to fix this, to keep her and his baby safe. But there was nothing he could do but hold her hand and comfort her. It was the worst spot he'd ever been in. Cam Sinclair was used to fixing things. That's what he did: he took charge and he fixed whatever needed to be fixed.

He couldn't fix this. It was a humbling and maddening place to be.

"Look at me, Lana. Look at me," his voice was hoarse with emotion. She opened her beautiful, beautiful eyes and he saw tears swirling there. "You are strong. Our baby is strong. We are going to get through this. Don't give up on me. Your attitude, our attitude matters." He lifted her hand and kissed it. "It matters."

She inhaled deeply, her expression pensive. "I know, you're right. I love you." She held his gaze and nodded then said softly, "We'll get through this, together."

CHAPTER SEVEN

Las Vegas, Nevada

Drake Sinclair sat in the stands of the crowded arena in Las Vegas on opening night of the National Finals Rodeo and waited for Vance to climb over the bar and settle onto the saddle of his first bronc ride. He could see Vance behind the chutes, pacing, ready. His brother had always lived to ride.

Maisy and Libby sat beside Drake, and he could see how nervous Libby was for Vance. But surprisingly to Drake, the young woman who'd seemed like a wreck when she'd first come to town and waitressed at Gert's café, dropping things every time Vance was in town and entered the café, was now fairly calm as she watched Vance prepare for his ride.

Maisy, who knew nothing about rodeo, on the other hand, was nervous and a bucket of questions. "So, he just loves to ride? He'd have to go through this nerve-racking enormous event."

She'd been questioning him since they'd arrived at the convention center and taken their seats.

"He does. He's probably not even thinking about how big the crowd is. His mind is already going over the ride in his head. All his focus is on that bronc. Besides, you love being on camera so I'm surprised you seem so nervous for him."

"I love being on camera but there is a big difference in what I do and this." She looked around at the stands, and up toward the top seats as if they reached to the moon. "This is overwhelming. There is just me and my camera and a small group if any when I do my show."

He was startled at Maisy's words. "The cooking

competition is going to have a lot of people in the crowd."

She laughed. "Not this many. Did you like this? Didn't all of you do rodeo?"

"Growing up we all had different things we were interested in and we all had varying times of infatuation and success. I had a little talent and determination in bronc riding—not saying I would have had Vance's success, because I didn't last long enough on the road to find out. I got out there and it didn't take me a year on the road before I knew my heart was back in Texas on the ranch. And with the family. I gave it up, walked away and never regretted it. It was similar with the others.

"He loves it though," Libby said, taking her eyes off of Vance for a moment to smile at them. "Absolutely loves it."

"Yes, he does, especially since you're with him." Drake smiled at her, glad she and Vance had met. "The thing is, Maisy, that road is a tough thing to wrestle with, almost harder to come to terms with. But chasing that golden buckle, which is what he'll win if he takes the championship, it takes a lot of road time and there is no getting around that. He might be nineteen hundred miles away from his next rodeo and the moment the one he's competing in is over, he's in the truck and driving so he can make it to the next spot. And he's not the only one doing it. Only the top fifteen make it to Vegas. And to get the score and wins to secure he's in that number means he goes like that almost from February to December. Only way he gets to come home is when a rodeo is close enough he has a day or two he can detour and stop by."

"Wow, I'm on the road with my show but that's triple the time I spend driving."

"Yeah, you understand to a point what he's enduring and how much he has to love riding saddle broncs to stay out there that much. Vance lives in that little travel trailer he pulls. It gets hard but, Libby choosing to be with him gave him wind under his sails."

Libby giggled at that and smiled at them again, her eyes lit with mischief. "That's sweet, Drake. I'm so glad you're my brother-in-law."

"Right back at you, Libby. And I believe you're going to bring him luck this year."

"I do too," Maisy agreed.

Libby had clasped her hands together beneath her chin as she watched Vance tug at his gloves one last time. "Oh, I hope so. I really, really do."

The announcer's voice rang out over the speaker. "Now let's give a hand to one of the cowboys out of Texas, Vance Presley on Hard Bit." He rattled off all of Vance's championships but they weren't listening; they were tuned in to Vance. He lifted his head their direction as the crowd cheered then he touched the brim of his hat grabbed the railing and in a quick movement climbed over and lowered himself onto the saddle.

"What's that thick rope he's holding called?" Maisy grabbed hold of Drake's arm.

Drake grinned. "The bronc rein. And that's all he can hold onto. He needs to hold it just right to help control the ride. Too loose and it's not good. His boots, watch his boots, those spurs need to be touching the bronc above its breast bone when the first buck happens or he's disqualified. And his free arm can't touch him or the bronc or he's disqualified."

The gate opened and the bronc busted from the chute as if it were an airplane. It flew up then with its head down; it landed hard on its front legs, butt high back legs kicking out behind it. Vance had perfect form and took the shock of the first buck as if it were nothing. His body was parallel to the bronc's, his spurs pointing to the ground; his head almost touched the bronc's hips. Libby and Maisy gasped but Drake knew it was going to be a good, wild eight seconds and it was and Vance showed that he'd come to win. When it was done and the buzzer sounded, he jumped to the ground, whipped his hat from his head and held it toward the roof as the crowd roared.

It was a fantastic ride and the score popped onto the monster screen hanging from the ceiling of the Thomas & Mack Center.

Drake surged to his feet, clapping hard. "Atta boy, Vance," he yelled, and gave Libby a thumbs-up when she turned happy eyes his way.

"That was a good score?" Maisy squealed.

"Yes, a great score," he told her and caught her as she threw her arms around his waist and jumped up and down. He laughed and wrapped his arm around her. "If he keeps that up, he's got a shot."

"I hope so." Libby said taking time away from hanging out over the railing screaming praise for Vance.

Drake's phone rang and Maisy dropped her arms allowing him room to reach for it, unclipping it from its holder on his hip. He glanced at the screen and saw it was Cam calling. "I better take this. I'll head up somewhere quieter and be right back."

"Okay," she said as he headed out of the stands. "We'll be here waiting."

He hurried up the steps toward the exit to the concourse. His thoughts had instantly gone to Lana, though there was a possibility Cam was checking on Vance's first ride of the week. "Hey, Cam," he said, as he made it to the landing and walked past the concession stands toward the far side and a corner area where some of the noise might be lower. "Is everything okay? Is Lana okay?"

"At the moment she's fine but she's in the hospital. She has preeclampsia."

Drake didn't know much about pregnant women but he knew for horse's preeclampsia or eclampsia were not good. "Is her blood pressure out of control?" He knew there were all kinds of complications that could happen.

"They're watching her closely. Monitoring her kidneys and her liver function. They don't want her pressure to spike because there's a danger of blood clots and brain injury. Look, bottom line is they're monitoring her and the baby constantly. The only way to fix it is to deliver the baby but the baby is only thirty-five weeks at this point and that's too early. We need to get her to thirty-seven weeks if possible. She won't make the full forty weeks but every week we can give the baby lowers her chance of having complications. But they have to monitor both of them and if either one of them starts to get worse, they'll take the baby."

Drake sank against the wall as he sorted through what his brother-in-law was telling him. "How bad?

Are you're telling me she or the baby could die?"

"Yeah." Cam's voice was gruff.

Drake's mind reeled. Panic wouldn't help anyone. "What can I do? We'll load up and be on the first flight out. Tell Lana we're on our way."

"No," Cam barked. "Sorry, didn't mean to snap but Lana knew that's what you'd say. She didn't want me to call. She insists that you don't tell Vance. She wants him to win and there isn't anything any of us can do."

"He will want to know. We can be there to support her emotionally. We can find better doctors—"

"Listen to me, Drake. You and I are a lot alike. We don't like not being in control and I'm telling you, everything you're thinking, everything going through your head, has already gone through mine. There is nothing you can do. Pray. And stay there and root your brother on and then get back here with him hopefully wearing that golden buckle. I'm serious, Drake. The last thing Lana needs is pressure. She needs her stress level to stay low, and her anxiety level. If she thinks Vance gave up his shot at the championship, it could harm her. She knows how good he just rode. We had just gotten moved from the emergency room to her room and she asked me to check the score before I came out in the courtyard to call you. Knowing he rode so well, even has a shot of winning the round tonight, made her smile and that's the first smile she's had since they rushed her to the hospital."

Drake's mind reeled. His mother's death had been on his mind from day one of Lana announcing she was having a baby. "I'll stay. I'll need to tell Vance, though. He'll never forgive me. He'll have to have the right to choose what he wants to do."

"But it might mess up his chances of winning."

"That's a chance I have to take. He has a right to know. You'd want to know."

He hesitated then a sigh sounded through the phone. "Yeah, you're right. But don't let him get on a plane. Make sure he knows that if he shows up here at the hospital, I'll stop him at the door. I'll do everything in my power to keep Lana from knowing he's not competing. And I mean that."

Drake heard the steel in Cam's words. "I'll let him

know. Did you call Dad?"

"Yeah, they're on their way, the whole Presley clan have made plans to get here. Rooms are being provided to all of you at the resort. So, there's a place for all of you when Vance rides the last ride of the rodeo."

"Thanks."

"And I forgot, she has a message for Maisy. She said to tell her to show them what Texans are made of and that she'll be watching."

"She wants Maisy to compete?" It was just like his stubborn sister to run the show from a hospital bed. "Maisy isn't going to be happy. She's going to be a mess worrying about Lana and Eva Marie."

"Tell her my wife, if we make it through the next two days safely, is going to need something to help take her mind off of worrying about the baby. Watching Maisy compete will be a huge help."

"You're right. I might not be able to do anything for you there but I can take care of this."

"I knew I could count on you. Thanks."

"Cam, keep my baby sister safe."

"I plan on doing everything I can to do that. I won't be leaving her side."

After they disconnected, Drake didn't move. So many emotions tangled inside him. He'd lived through the nightmare of losing his mom. He'd been the oldest and had aged that night by ten years. He'd helped hold his family together through it all and he didn't want to have a replay of that horrible time again. He'd been angry at God for a long time, until he realized it was God helping them get through it.

Taking a deep breath, he sent a prayer up for his sister and baby niece and then he headed back to find Maisy and Libby before they went to find Vance.

CHAPTER EIGHT

Fear had clung to Lana since being admitted to the hospital but she'd decided that the best thing she could do for Eva Marie was to stay as calm as possible and to do everything the doctors told her to do.

She'd spent many hours prior to being admitted to the hospital dealing with feelings and emotions that were like a roller coaster, from joy at the thought of her baby to dark worries about dying like her mother had done and leaving her baby motherless. Now, she knew she needed to keep her stress level down and she realized that she was focusing on that…on doing anything and everything she could to stay positive so hopefully it would have a good effect on her body and what it was going through. And she had an abundance of help as all of the Sinclair women and men came to see her to check on her and to show her love.

How blessed she was to have them.

"Cam, you didn't look comfortable sleeping on that couch last night. Not that you slept much. I'd tell you to go home and sleep but I know you won't."

"I slept fine. And no, I won't be going home. How are you feeling?"

"I'm not hurting and I'm not feeling dizzy."

"That's good." He placed his hand on the baby. "How's this little lady doing?"

"She moving so that's good. I think she seems fine. You were here when the doctor came in and checked everything."

"I know, but I figure it doesn't hurt to ask you." He kissed her temple. "So, there is a herd of Presleys and Sinclairs out there overflowing in the waiting room. Doc says there is no way all of them are getting in here to see you at one time."

Her heart swelled with love for all of them as she imagined how the waiting room must look. She couldn't believe that they were all here. Her dad and Karla had flown in late during the night and had gotten to come in and see her already. Karla had been pleased with her care and that reassured both she and Cam that she was in good hands, though they'd already felt like her doctor was good. Though Adam, Cam's cousin, hadn't been in to see her yet, he had done some checking and consulted with Cam that the hospital and the doctor were highly thought of.

"But I want to see them."

"I know, and I think it will help keep you occupied and your stress level down. What do you think—we're going to go in shifts?"

"That would be great. I want to watch Maisy compete. She is competing, right?"

"Yes, I told Drake what you said and he is taking care of that."

Relief filled her. "Good. I was so worried they would rush back here."

"He was going to but now he's making sure they

stay. So, as long as it doesn't stress you out, I was thinking maybe your dad and brothers could come tonight and we could watch his second round together."

"I would love that. I might stress, but if I start to, y'all can go to the lobby and then come back and tell me. I am so thrilled he won last night."

"It was a great ride. If you're doing good, I'm going to tag team and go have breakfast in the cafeteria with everyone crammed in the waiting room who I can talk into taking a break. And Mom and Jillian want to come in and bring you breakfast. How is that?"

"It's good. I'm glad you're getting out of here for a bit. Tell everyone I appreciate them so much. Eva Marie is going to have the most wonderful, huge family of people who love her."

He cupped her cheek. "Yes, she is. Tomorrow, if all your vitals are still good, you're going to have company watching Maisy compete. She knows you're going to be watching, so we're going to sneak all the women in the family in here and y'all can have a watching party and cheer Maisy on."

"Wonderful. I guess if I was going to have a scary time in the hospital, I picked a great two weeks to do it." She was being positive and at least that was true. It kept some of the fear at bay and that was a good thing.

"Yeah, you just keep those thoughts focused, babe. We're all going to work as a team to support you."

She blinked hard, fighting back emotions that hit her. "I love you."

"That's what I live for." His eyes, so tender, caressed her face. "Enjoy breakfast."

She watched him leave and breathed deeply. Just him being out of the room seemed to take some of her strength with him. She'd come to rely heavily on his strong shoulders. But before she could think much more, the door opened and Violet came into the room, followed by Jillian.

"We are here to check on you for ourselves." Violet set the tray she was carrying on the rolling tray and then came to her side and took her hands. "Let me look at you." She smiled sincerely as she took Lana in with caring eyes. She nodded slowly. "You're a brave woman, and a determined one, I can tell. I want to say something to you. I knew that when my Cam finally fell in love, it would have to be with a woman with a strength and a stubborn streak that could challenge his. I knew this because he always had a mind of his own. Always knew what he wanted and where he belonged."

She smiled and patted Lana's hands. "He was born a Floridian but almost immediately knew his heart was in Texas. And then you came along. I knew that God worked in mysterious ways to bring you two together. You're perfect together. I'm telling you this because I just know the two of you can get through anything and you're going to get through this. Together. And you have all of us as your cheer squad. We're here for you, my love. And I'm so happy you're going to be my granddaughter's mother."

"You're going to be okay," Jillian added, patting her shoulder.

Tears pricked again and she blinked damp lashes. "Thank you. Because I need you."

Jillian gave her a tender smile. "Us mothers have to stick together."

"And Lana," Violet said, "I haven't ever told you how very sorry I am that you lost your mother. I can only imagine how much you must miss her during this time. I know I would have ached for my mom if I hadn't had her during the births of all of my babies, so my heart goes out to you and all who share a similar loss."

Her throat ached. She'd been putting on a happy face like a bandage, trying to hold in her pain to protect her baby. She'd somehow thought in doing that that no one would dig deep. That everyone would let her continue to try to hide what she was feeling. But not Violet. She'd zeroed directly in and was exposing it.

Her tender smile touched Lana. "I hope you know we are here for you. Not just for you to smile and pretend you don't hurt...but for you to share your deepest fears and aches, and burdens. That's what mothers do. I'd like to stand in the gap for your mother if you'll let me. Not be her, but to give you the love and the soft place to land that she would have been if she were still here physically. I know she's with you in your heart. I know you have women in Ransom Creek who stood in for her, your aunt Trudy for one. I'd like to be there for you too."

Lana hugged Violet. Violet wrapped her arms around Lana and hugged her tightly. And she breathed in the scent of cinnamon and vanilla, scents that she could imagine her mother smelling of after having baked cookies for all of her brothers. The fear she'd stuffed down deep sometime during the night when she'd told herself that was what she needed to do surged forward but it didn't overtake her; it seemed to ease some.

"It's always easier when you have someone to share your burden with." Violet smiled at her. "I know if you and Cam are like me and Sam, you are being strong for each other. And that's a good thing. But I'm here for you and so is Jillian."

"I am. We all are. Girl power is a good thing."

"Thank you. I'm so scared and trying not to be. But this has helped. I know Cam is struggling, worrying about me and the baby. But he wouldn't show me and I'm trying not to show him because I don't want him to worry any more than he already is."

"I'm the same way." Jillian uncovered the plate of homemade cinnamon rolls and smiled. "Mom asked me what I thought you'd want for breakfast and I told her to make a comfort food. And nothing she makes is more comforting than her cinnamon rolls."

Lana's heart eased up for a moment. "Those smell like heaven."

"I agree." She put one on a plate and handed it to her. "We love you, Lana."

"Yes, we do." Violet took the roll Jillian handed her.

"I love you too."

Jillian bit into her roll and smiled. "What about me?"

"You too." And then she bit into the gooey cinnamon roll and just let the scents and taste of love seep through her.

Cam had shared his worries over Lana struggling with depression and that she hadn't actually told him she was but that he knew she was having extreme feelings of missing her mother. They'd immediately jumped in to help and this morning's visit he hoped helped her. When he returned to the room, he could tell that his mother had used some of her motherly magic on Lana. There seemed to be a little less worry around her eyes and the tightness of her mouth.

The room smelled amazing and he had been more than thrilled they'd saved him one of his mom's cinnamon rolls. Then, that evening, her dad, Brice, Shane, and Cooper, and his dad and Jake gathered with them to watch Vance win his second night of riding. While as many of the rest of his family, including Adam who was still in town, gathered out at Max's house and watched. Though none of them were particular rodeo fans they wanted to see Lana's brother ride in the championship. And once again he had a good night, Vance was on fire and made riding a bucking saddle bronc look easy. Though he knew there was nothing about it that was easy. He won again and when interviewed after it was announced he told Lana the ride was for her.

Drake called her from Vegas afterwards, and he and Vance both spoke with her. She hadn't wanted Vance to know but Drake had warned him that he'd told him. Vance seemed more determined than ever to win, but told her he'd come to Windswept Bay that night if she needed him or wanted him to. She'd insisted he stay and compete.

The family was united around them and that gave Cam comfort.

His dad took him aside before everyone left. "Son, you should have told us you were worried. You know if you need anything, all you have to do is ask."

"I know, Dad, and I'm sorry. I just thought…that I could handle it on my own. But, I'm grateful to have your support now. Thanks for your support now." He hugged his dad.

Cam had always tried to handle everything himself. But he was realizing that it was okay to let his family in to share some of his burden.

CHAPTER NINE

Las Vegas, Nevada

Drake and Libby sat in the audience of the cooking show studio and watched Maisy. They were nervous while she looked ready to take on the world.

"Okay, contestants, your challenge is to gather your ingredients for some down-home comfort food with a twist of something fast food to finish it off. You'll have forty-five minutes to finish this challenge and the winner gets to return to compete in the kitchen war episode where the prize is a try-out for a show of your very own." The judge grinned at the wide-eyed contestants then looked straight at Maisy who was smiling at the crowd and giving the viewers at home a thumbs up sign. "Maisy Love you look like you're ready to rock and roll on this."

Maisy's eyes twinkled. "Chef Allen, I love to cook so I'm always ready."

He laughed. "From watching some of your test videos prior to the show I have to agree. So, everyone the timer is set. Go."

Everyone scattered. Maisy took her basket and headed straight to the freezer and grabbed a container of vanilla ice-cream. Then dashed to snag some large onions, a bag of thick sliced bread, some eggs, cheese, and a few other ingredients.

Chef Allen trailed her. "Interesting combination you've got there, Maisy."

"I'm all about interesting." She moved to the workstation and set the ice cream on the counter then all her other ingredients as the other contestants made it back to their workstations too.

"Before I head over and bother the other contestants tell us what all this is going to create."

Drake had already figured it out by this time. It was something she'd made for him one evening when she'd cooked at his home. The judges were in for a treat.

"Well, it's one of my favorite dishes. And my fiancé's too. He's a tough Texas cowboy and this won him over so maybe it'll win the judges over, too." She glanced at Drake and winked. "It's a Monte Cristo ham and cheese sandwich, a real down-home comfort food that could be paired with homemade tomato soup or French onion soup but my fast food restaurant twist is to-die-for homemade hand battered fried onion rings."

"You officially have my attention." Chef Allen lit up the camera with a grin. "Make a little extra would you or I might have to toss a judge and slide into a judging seat."

Maisy laughed as he headed off to visit with the others and then she smiled at the judges who were looking really interested, and then she went to work.

"It sounds good," Libby whispered.

"It is." Drake could honestly say that he had had this sandwich and it was amazing but what was more amazing was what Maisy Love could do with an onion ring. Melt in your mouth, perfectly fried, perfectly spiced with some secret ingredient and some secret batter sauce. She was going to give them a tough dish to beat.

"She looks good," Lily said looking at him with tension on her face but sparkling eyes.

"I'm so excited for her. She doesn't even look nervous."

"Nope. She is in her element." And he knew she was.

Maisy Love was a natural. She smiled into the camera and his heart went weak. That woman could melt him from a mile away, and he knew that as she worked people across America were rooting for her. They couldn't help themselves because there was just something about Maisy that made you want to stand up and cheer for her. Her internet show was that way. He knew this because he had watched every episode. Yup, him the rough tough cowboy had sat and watched the love of his life charm people on her YouTube channel, cooking and interacting with her guests as she traveled across Texas or wherever she had gone to make those episodes. Truth was, though she could cook, it was more than that that made the show a success. Maisy adored what she did and the love of talking with other cooks and highlighting their talent caused her personality to bubble and overflow, thus charming the camera and the audience watching. She truly enjoyed her guests and was amazing at bringing out their best for viewers.

Today her competitors didn't stand a chance.

They were all busy working at their stations. One contestant, Ramona, seemed suddenly to have lost something and began frantically looking over her station. "Where's my eggs? Oh my goodness I've forgotten to get my eggs."

One of the rules of this particular show was that once you were at your station you could not go after more ingredients.

"How many do you need?" Maisy called across the room.

Ramona jerked around. "Four."

Maisy's dish required several eggs and she'd grabbed seven. Drake had counted earlier as she'd set them out. He'd taken in all her ingredients. She'd already cracked three eggs and had one in her hand ready to crack. Without hesitating she gathered the other three and rushed them over to Ramona who was clearly stressed.

"Oh, thank you," Ramona gasped. "Is that acceptable to the rules?"

Maisy smiled. "Neighbors being neighborly is always acceptable, right, Chef Allen?"

"The lady knows her rules. Yes, Maisy Love, that is acceptable."

Drake was proud of Maisy and her giving spirit but now he was worried that she didn't have enough egg mixture to coat her sandwiches enough. He watched on the edge of his seat as she returned to her station and went back to work. The only sign she was feeling a touch of stress was when she swiped the back of her wrist across her forehead.

"Ramona, are you having fun?" she called as she

began dipping her sandwiches in the mixture.

"I'm frazzled, not going to lie," Ramona called. "I bake but never against a clock."

The other two contestants were busy and barely acknowledging anything else going on around them as they worked to win.

Maisy placed a sandwich in the sizzling pan. "That timer is ticking but all you need to do is ignore it and get your natural rhythm going. I love cooking anytime, to a timer or dance music. Do you ever dance while you're in the kitchen?" Holding a sandwich Maisy backed away from the counter, did a twist and spin before sashaying back and dropping her sandwich into the egg batter. "Show me some moves, girlfriend," Maisy sang and Ramon laughed.

And then the older woman did a sudden quick step and a spin then got back to work.

"See there, fun is the real name of the game," Maisy said as Ramona smiled at her.

"Thank you for the reminder."

"She's amazing," Libby said. "I knew she would do that. That's just who she is. "When I was on her show I was a nervous wreck. But she calmed me down and she actually got me to enjoy it and I never thought I would. But I actually had fun. It's just amazing watching her. She could totally do this every week on a nationally televised show like this. And you can bet that just like it did for Vance, knowing Lana is in the hospital watching is going to fire her up to do extra good. Look at her smiling and dancing. I can only imagine that Lana is laughing too right now."

He agreed with everything Libby said. If given the chance, Maisy would probably have a hit network show. And today, for Lana she was dazzling the audience and the judges, he hoped. But he knew his sister had to be smiling back at the hospital. And that brought him to thoughts of their future. He'd do anything for Maisy even move if something like this made her happy. When they were married he'd give up working on the ranch everyday if they needed to move to make her dreams come true. The time was ticking away and Maisy had poured the now melted ice cream into a bowl, stirred it then cut her onions into large rings. She worked quickly to toss the raw onions into the bowl with the ice cream then took them out one at a time and dredged them through the flour mixture and dropped them carefully into the coconut oil to fry. His mouth watered thinking about how delicious they were going to be.

Moments later Chef Allen called out, "Alright, contestants, time's almost up. Five seconds, four, three, two, one. Time's up." All hands lifted in the air as the competition was over.

Drake looked across the room at her plate of food and his mouth watered, it looked fantastic, deliciously golden finger-licking-good. In the next moments, the celebrity chef judges were delivered their plates and the look in their eyes, except for the poker-faced man on the end, said they liked what they saw. Jed, a very serious looking older man wearing a bow tie, closed his eyes and just let the Monte Cristo sandwich melt in his mouth. Then he picked up an onion ring, didn't say a word as he dipped it in a mixture of ketchup and whatever else she had mixed in for the sauce that made that sauce so delicious, and then he took a bite.

Meanwhile, the female judge, preppy with spiked white hair and ruby red lipstick picked up her sandwich and took a small bite—but quickly took another bite. She set it aside and then picked up the onion ring. Her eyes sparkled as she chewed on that onion ring and looked at the judge beside her. Connor gave him a wow look before she took another bite of the onion ring.

Poker-faced judge owned several top restaurant chains across America and his expression never changed as he took his bite of the sandwich—Drake did not appreciate his lack of expression. He wanted to know what the guy was thinking and what was wrong with showing emotion?

The guy gave away nothing as he picked up the onion ring dipped it in the sauce and placed it carefully into his mouth. He set down the onion ring and dusted his fingertips. Drake felt like yanking the man up and demanding that he give Maisy some appreciation. Who could take only one bite? One bite took restriction that bordered on too tight to be right—

"Drake, you look like you're going to go yank that guy up and toss him across the room." Libby giggled.

"What?" Drake stared at Libby and only then realized she was probably right since his face felt tight, strained. He tried to relax. Truth was he wanted to get up and pace the room. He hadn't been this nervous since watching Vance in his third run last night at the NFR. He'd won three nights in a row and it had been inspiring and well deserved. Now Drake wanted Maisy to get the win that she deserved.

Chef Allen stepped up. "Well, judges, what's your verdict?"

The first judge, both hands on the table, looked straight at Maisy. "I do not know what you did to this plate but this was excellent. Those onion rings are fabulous. Did I see you using ice cream?"

Maisy smiled. "What better way to add fast food appeal than to use soft serve ice cream batter made for fast food ice cream machines to make another fast food item like the onion ring?"

All the judges smiled, including poker-face.

Judge One nodded. "Very well done. This was excellent, one of the best meals I've ever had on the show."

The second judge picked up an onion ring and pointed it at Maisy. "I will follow you around the country to eat these. And they are perfect with this sandwich. Which by the way is outstanding. Well done. Your competitors are going to have to step up their game I can tell you that."

Judge Poker Face picked up the sandwich looked at the inside then looked at Maisy. "I don't know if you realize, but this is one of our specialties at my restaurants. And I'll tell you this Monte Cristo sandwich is the best I've ever had. I might even have to take mine off the menu after this. And the onion ring is golden flaky perfection."

"Well, I'll be amazed," Cam muttered, breathing a sigh of relief.

"She might win," Libby gushed beside him.

As far as he was concerned she already had won,

no matter whether the judges said she had or not. Because he knew in a hospital room in Windswept Bay, his sweet sister was watching and hopefully smiling as Maisy helped distract her from the many fears that were probably knocking at her heart. And that made him love Maisy even more than he already did.

CHAPTER TEN

Laying in the hospital bed, her hand resting on her belly, feeling her baby moving, Lana looked around the room. Everyone had joined Lana to watch Maisy on the cooking show. Since she'd been admitted, the room had been transformed with Christmas decorations but the best decoration of all were the family surrounding her.

All of them were here, all of them had taken off work to be here. It was humbling to look around and know they'd all come. Her family and Cam's family...their family. Cali, Shar, Olivia, Jillian, Lily,

Sammy Joe, and then all the way from Texas her brothers and dad had come along with Karla, Beth, Jenna, and Tara. And Cam's mother, Violet, was here also and she and Karla were sitting on the couch visiting and getting to know each other while the younger women congregated around the room talking with each other and with Lana. And then there was Aunt Trudy who had jumped on Gage's private jet also. She'd relayed the messages from Sally Ann and Gert, that they were praying for her and would be coming to see her next week. The little room was packed with love. And Lana was thankful that after they'd promised the nurses that they'd leave after the show ended they'd been permitted to stay for the show.

"She's going to do this. Those other three contestants don't stand a chance," Shar said with decisive certainty. "I'd hate to see me up there, you know I can't cook."

The room erupted with laughter.

"You never cook," her brother Jake called out amid the teasing laughter.

"It's okay, she's too busy saving sea turtles and

that's fine with me," Gage said from where he was leaning against the wall talking to his half-brother, BJ. Lana liked Gage and BJ and thought Shar's and Olivia's husbands were perfect matches for them. She wondered again if there was going to be any surprise baby news soon from Gage and Shar.

"It takes more than just being able to cook to be up there," Olivia pointed out. "What do you think if she were to get a show. Do you think your brother would give up his ranch?"

Lana considered that question, her thoughts swinging to her mother in a sudden impact. Drake knew what it was to have love one moment and to lose it the next. "Drake loves her and he loves the ranch. But I wouldn't put it past him to do whatever it took to give Maisy her dream—if that is her dream."

"Although we get the cart before the horse and remember that tonight she just needs to win. They don't just hand out cooking shows like candy."

"True," Aunt Trudy harrumphed. "But we're partial to her and think they'd be crazy not to."

"I agree," Beth said. "Still, if she wins this show

she will get the chance."

"I don't mean to be rude, what she's fixing is like unbelievable. It sounds simple but it's not. She just does something to food, I don't know, maybe it's an addition of love or something but she could cook for me all the time."

Lily chuckled. "Me too. I like peanut butter and you all know this girl don't cook. Poor Trent did not marry me for my cooking skills."

"No, he didn't." Kelsey laughed, nudging Lily with her elbow. "You two get along like monkeys in a tree though, so all is well."

"Look, there's Drake and Libby. I guess Vance is practicing for tonight," Aunt Trudy said, clapping her hands together. "Doesn't he look like he's just in love watching her from all the way out there in the audience?"

"He does," Violet agreed as the show went to commercials. "Trudy and Karla, I think our boys and our girls have all done very well by themselves finding true love. I mean it's evident on all of the faces, don't you agree?"

Lana looked around the room and had to agree. They were all lucky to have each other and she was lucky to have all of them. What a humongous group when you put all the Presleys and all the Sinclairs together.

"Lana," Cali asked. "What are you thinking about?"

"About how lucky I am. Look at all of you. You're here for me, I mean, you're here for me and for Eva Marie and Cam. I'm just so lucky to have so many of you." She laughed as tears sprang to her eyes, tears of gratitude. "My baby is going to be so lucky to have all of you in her life."

Shar came over to stand beside her. "She's going to be lucky to have you as her mother too."

"Yes, she is," Jillian said as others agreed, looking at her with love.

Lana couldn't speak for a moment and was grateful that that the show came back on and everyone focused on it and the finale. The judges brought the contestants in for one more question before they awarded the prize. Each contestant told what had inspired them to love cooking.

All the competitors were heartfelt but when it came to Maisy, she smiled and looked at the camera and waved gently. "Hi, Lana. Everyone, Lana is my very dear friend and almost sister-in-law, and she was just admitted to the hospital on bed rest until her baby comes around Christmas time. We wanted to be with her. But she *forced* me to compete and she's watching right now. So, though there were many things that caused me to love to cook, tonight I cooked to entertain Lana. I'm hoping she's not stressing out over if I won or didn't win. Because, Lana, no matter what happens, I'm about to be an almost aunt and that's a win every way I look at it." She looked back at the judges. "So, that wasn't exactly what brought me to this stage today but it's what kept me here."

Lana placed her hand over her heart, deeply touched by Maisy's words.

"Well, it turns out your soon to be sister-in-law knew something we didn't know until now, you are an excellent chef and the winner of the Roving Chefs Cooking Competition."

The room burst into clapping and excited conversation. The nurse had to poke her head in the door and ask them to calm down. Immediately they complied and looked at Lana.

"We didn't get you too excited did we," Cooper asked. "You feel okay?"

Lana chuckled. "I actually feel better than I've felt in a really long time. Thank you all for coming and sharing this with me. I'm so happy for Maisy, and Eva Marie is very calm right now. So, who knows, maybe she will grow up to be a chef like her aunt Maisy. I sure hope Maisy and Drake set the date soon so she is officially Aunt Maisy to Eva Marie and an official part of the family."

Cam touched her stomach and smiled at her. "I'm sure it will happen when they are ready. They're going to have some major decisions to make now that she's won that competition."

"I can't imagine the ranch without Drake," Shane said. "I've grown comfortable with Dad being involved less."

"Hey," her dad said. "You're glad to get rid of

me?"

Everyone laughed. Shane shook his head, a smile on his lips. "No, but you deserve some time off and so it's a natural thing for you to hand the reins over to all of us more. To Drake. He's the one who naturally stepped into your roll."

Brice jumped in, "Not that we can't cope if he ends up moving or whatever he does depending on if more comes from this win for Maisy. We'd be happy for him, but we like the way it is."

"Yes we do," Cooper added. "But we'd do whatever it took to make our women happy." He looped an arm around Beth and kissed her lips when she smiled up at him.

"Even let me finally put you in my calendar with my dressed-up goats?" she smiled wickedly and his brows dipped.

"I walked right into that didn't I?"

"You did, but maybe I'll let you off the hook because you know, we women would do anything for our men too. So, y'all need to relax and not write your brother out of the picture just yet. They will get their life together figured out. Just like Libby and Vance are doing."

"I married a very brilliant lady," Cooper said and hugged her close while looking around the room at his brothers.

"I agree with Beth," Lana said. "Besides, you all know Drake, he will put a lot of thought and planning into everything he does. He doesn't do anything on the spur of the moment."

Her dad crossed his arms and nodded, agreeing with her words. "That's not always the right thing to do though. He might just need to do what his heart tells him is right. And whatever that is, we will all be happy for him. Now, its time for us to get out of here and let Lana rest. Are you feeling okay, honey?"

Lana took the hand he held out to her and she squeezed hard. Oh, how she loved her daddy. "I am. Just starting to get tired as the excitement of Maisy's win winds down. I might sleep. But make sure y'all keep Cam informed about Vance's ride later tonight. He can tell me how he did when I wake up."

"We will," her dad said.

Cam stood at the door and thanked each one of her family and his as they left, after each one gave her a hug. By the time they were all gone Lana was really tired, even though it was only around eight-thirty. The baking cook-off had been early evening which as it was turning out was a very good thing.

Cam came over and cupped her face in his hands and leaned close. "I've been thinking a lot lately and was going to share this later but after all the talk about Drake and Maisy I think now is a good time. I love you, Lana Sinclair. And just so you know, I would move anywhere you needed me to move if it made you happy. You know that, right?" He kissed her lips gently then pulled back, swallowed hard. "I'm thinking it would be nice to buy some land with a house near Ransom Creek and make that our home. What do you think? Would you like to raise our family near your family, let our children and all of your brothers' children grow up close and you'd get to be near everyone you love?"

Lana's eyes widened and her mouth, her beautiful mouth fell slightly open but no sound came out.

He frowned. "You don't like the idea? We don't have—"

"No, I do. I love the idea. Oh Cam, if it's really an option, and you could be happy then I would love to move back near my family and let Eva Marie…and our other children if we are so blessed, grow up surrounded by love."

"Then it's a done deal. Just so you know, I'm happy wherever you are. And don't you ever forget it, darlin'."

And then he lowered his lips to hers and kissed her with all the love of a man who had it all.

Three days later her blood pressure began spiking.

CHAPTER ELEVEN

It all happened quickly. Everything had seemed fine and they were into the second week of the hospital stay when Lana began feeling bad and the nurses monitoring her and their baby became concerned. Cam hadn't slept much in the time they'd been in the hospital, never staying in the reclining chair when the nurses came in to check on Lana or to take her blood samples. He took care of Lana as much as possible, wanting to give her as much comfort as he could, and needing the connection to her during this time. He got used to knowing what her vital signs were on the constantly beeping monitors hooked up to her and the baby. And tonight they were higher than normal. He was concerned and not sleeping at all.

Lana was resting though restless. And he decided to walk the short distance down the hall to the coffee station. He was pouring his coffee when he heard a call go out over the loud speaker and heard a commotion down the hall as the voice on the loudspeakers called out Lana's room number. He set the coffee pot on the counter and ran.

Lana and his baby were in trouble.

He was pacing the waiting room when their families began arriving.

"What's happening," Max asked as he and Kelsey came rushing down the hall followed by his cousin Adam and many of his family and Lana's family. They all gathered around him. His hands were shaking as he stared at them, the pit of his stomach rolled.

"She had a placental abruption," he quoted what the doctor had quickly told him was going on before they'd whisked Lana down the hall to surgery. He'd barely had time to kiss her and all he could remember right now was the fear in her eyes and the way she'd clung to his hands.

"What is that?" Cali asked first as others echoed with the same question.

"It's…" Cam's words broke off as he thought of the blood. His gaze landed on Adam.

Adam stepped around everyone and placed his hand on Cam's shoulder. "It's where the placenta separates partially or completely from the inner wall of the uterus. It causes heavy bleeding for the mother and can block the oxygen supply to the baby. They need to act fast and get the baby out and stop the bleeding."

"Thank you," Cam said, grateful to have his cousin there who understood what was going on.

His mother rushed from the group and wrapped her arms around him. And while she hugged him, Cam saw Lana's dad and Karla rushing into the waiting room.

"What's happening? How is Lana," Marcus demanded.

"Dad," Shane said, as he and Brice moved toward

their dad. Cam knew that despite the fact that he'd had a heart attack almost two years earlier and had been doing good they still worried that he could have another one.

"She's in surgery," Brice offered. "Can you repeat what you just told us, Adam?"

"Of course," Adam said and did so.

Karla, being a nurse understood more than most standing in the room and she reached for Marcus's hand. "Thank goodness they were here at the hospital already. That helped cut down on the time."

"Yes," Adam agreed. "She's in good hands, Cam. They're going in now, doing what's best for both Lana and your baby girl."

Cam raked a hand through his hair. "I was supposed to be in there during the delivery but they took her away, and she looked scared when I had to let go of her hands as they took her behind the doors to the surgery area." His heart thundered and her eyes burned into his soul. "I should have demanded to go back there with her." He'd stood there and stared at those closed doors until one of the nurses had told him to wait in the waiting room.

Adam's jaw tightened and Cam caught the new tension in him. "There was nothing you could do back there. They need to act fast and the—" He glanced around then his gaze mellowed with compassion. "There could be more complications. They're trying to save your wife and baby's life. The doctor was thinking only of that when he left you behind."

Something about what Adam said seemed personal. Cam pulled back some of the anger that had been gathering in his gut at being left behind with only the terror in Lana's eyes.

"I'd have held her hand through anything. She needed me in there." He glared at Adam.

His cousin looked stricken before he nodded. "I see your point. It might not be long before they come through those same doors to tell you to come see your baby and your wife."

"He's right," Violet said softly. "You're upset but they truly are trying to save your family's lives."

He looked back to tell Adam he didn't mean to lash out at him but he'd already moved away and Cam couldn't find him in the crowded room.

His phone rang and he reached into his pocket and saw it was Drake. He stepped away from everyone and moved to the window as he answered the call.

"Cam, how is Lana? How are you? Dad called and we're going to book plane reservations"

"No," Cam growled, holding on to what he knew Lana would want. "Drake, I need you to keep Vance competing. He has two more rides. He can't quit. Lana wouldn't want it."

Drake growled in frustration on the other end of the line. "Cam, we can't stay here in Vegas when Lana might be in danger."

Cam raked a hand through his hair and rubbed, knowing he was making a mess of it but feeling so frustrated it didn't matter. "Look I know you want to be here. I understand it. But I have to level with you, Drake. I'm worried about Lana. But I am trying to hold it together and right now the only thing I know for certain is that Lana wants Vance competing. He has tonight and tomorrow and then y'all can come here and meet your new niece and give Lana a big hug. She's going to come through this and if you get on that plane and show up here this evening she's going to be sad that she caused Vance to miss out of another shot at the championship."

"Hang on," Drake said. He heard someone say something muffled on the other end of the line and then he heard Drake talking but not to him.

"Cam, it's Vance. I'm not sure I can compete knowing my sister is in danger."

Heart threatening to bust out of his chest Cam's hand tightened on the phone so hard he expected it to explode at any moment. "Vance, don't get on a plane yet. The doctor is going to come out any minute and tell me Lana and Eva Marie are okay. When he does that, you'll know she's okay and you'll be able to finish winning that golden buckle for you and for her."

There was silence on the other end of the line. "Okay, I'll do this for Lana. And I'm counting on her being okay. It's just we feel stuck out here and we're worried about her. I've been riding hard every night but I'm not happy about it, Cam. I'd rather be there."

Cam had known watching Vance ride last night that he was having a hard time after he'd come in third for the night and he probably felt like he'd let Lana down. But Lana had just felt bad for him, not let down. "I get what your feeling. But you can hug her in two days. With or without that buckle. She'll love you and be glad to see you no matter what. But she doesn't want to be the reason you miss out on your shot at the championship."

Vance sighed. "I'll stay and compete. We're booking a flight out as soon as the final ride.

"Vance, I'll call you back. The doctor just came out." Cam shut the call down and strode across the room to meet the doctor. He searched the doctor's expression as their eyes met. "How are they?"

The doctor stopped in front of him. "Cam, they're fine." He smiled. "Your wife and your daughter are safe. Would you like to see them? Lana is still coming out of anesthesia but I'd like you to hold your little girl for a few minutes so she can bond with you. How does that sound?"

Cam fought tears as emotion welled inside him. "Yes," he said, accepting his mom's hug and then numerous others from his sisters.

"Kiss our baby for us," his mom said.

"Congratulations, son. Now go," his dad said as the doctor headed back toward the doors that Cam had been thinking about busting down. "Give then our love."

To the well wishes of their families Cam strode after the doctor. At the door, he spun. "Someone call Vance and tell him the news. Tell him I'll send them pictures soon."

And then he walked through the doors the doctor was holding open for him and then followed him down the hall and into the delivery room.

Walking through that door and seeing Lana laying peacefully sleeping, alive and well and seeing his baby under the warming light, small but healthy was the most precious gift he could have ever received.

He went to where Lana slept, her eyes closed

looking peaceful. His heart surged with love and he couldn't wait for her to wake up so she could hold Eva Marie.

"If you'll unbutton your shirt so we can get a little skin-on-skin touch between you and your baby I'll hand her over," a nurse said, smiling as she held his very small, diaper clad baby girl out to him.

He quickly did as instructed, unable to take his eyes off of Eva Marie as the nurse gently laid her against his chest and he cupped his hands securely around her and felt her tiny heart beating against his.

"Hello, my little darlin'," he said softly, looking at his baby snuggled against him and then he glanced at Lana and saw her eyes flutter and then open. "Lana, honey, look who wants to meet you." He held Eva Marie close and bent to kiss his wife's forehead and to let her focus on their baby.

"Oh, Cam, she's beautiful and okay? Is she okay?" Her eyes closed again and a tear slipped down her cheek.

"She's okay, Lana. And you're okay. You did great. Now rest."

She smiled, opened her eyes briefly and then the anesthesia pulled her back. It would take a little more time before she was fully awake, but he was glad he'd been able to reassure her for now.

Everything was good. His world was complete and for the first time in months, Cam let himself relax and enjoy the moment.

He kissed Lana's soft lips once more and watched them curve into a gentle smile.

Dear Lord, how he loved this woman and this child. Life couldn't get any better than this.

Adam stood outside the hospital, his hands wrapped like a vise around the railing as he remembered why he couldn't go back into a trauma unit. He'd once thought, believed he'd been born to be a doctor. It had been his passion to achieve that goal for as long as he could remember. But, now, he didn't know what he wanted. Didn't know if he ever wanted to walk back into a hospital. He'd come to spend time with his cousins, he'd just been drawn to spend time with them, and they'd talked many evenings, late into the night about things they'd experienced and about the new direction they were taking their lives since leaving the military. And that was it, in many ways Adam had felt recently, not like he was working a hospital trauma unit but in a war zone.

"Adam," Max said behind him.

He turned and his cousin put his hands on his hips and smiled. "I saw you leave and wanted to check on you and to tell you that Eva Marie is here and both mother and baby are doing fine. Cam is with them now."

"Good to know." Adam breathed a sigh of relief. He'd been more worried than he'd let anyone know. He knew how quickly things could turn bad...but maybe that was just the perspective he'd begun to have lately. "Max, thanks for all your and Kelsey's hospitality. "I just wanted to tell you that. I'm going to come up and say my goodbyes. It's time for me to go home."

Max's lips firmed. "So you decided to go take that job?"

"No, I'm not ready to take on small–town physician yet. But, one thing I've realized since spending time with all of you is that I need to go reconnect with my own family. I wasn't ready when I came here, I had too much going on in my head. But now, I'm ready. I'm going to find a little shack on the beach like you did and remodel it while I figure things out and reconnect with everyone."

"It helped me. Nothing like working with your hands to give your mind time to mull things over. Trent did the same thing, just with tree houses."

"Thanks, you're a good man, Max. And you've found a good woman to share your life with."

"Maybe it's time you start looking for your own good woman."

Adam let his mind linger on that thought for an instant then shook his head. "I'm not ready for that. Not yet."

Max cocked his head to the side. "Maybe you're right. But, don't keep shutting your heart down. There are times for that and we've been there, but if you're starting over, don't shut that option out. I almost did and it would have been the worst mistake of my life."

"I'll think about it. But first, let's go up so I can say my goodbyes and congratulate everyone."

Max stepped forward and gave him a hug. "I'll be here for you if you need anything," he said then stepped back and they walked back into the hospital together.

Adam felt a sense of anticipation now that he'd made his mind up. He was going home, just down the Florida coast to Sunset Bay. Aptly named since his plan was to let the sun set on his past and hopefully find a new direction. He was looking for a sunrise.

He was looking for peace…and hopefully home was where he'd find it.

CHAPTER TWELVE

The day after being released from the hospital everyone gathered at Gage and Shar's house to celebrate the birth of Eva Marie and finally, their early Christmas before all of Lana's family headed back to Texas. Lana had been delighted when they'd arrived. Gage had gone overboard decorating the outside of the house with enough lights that she was sure could be seen from outer space. Lana was still having to take it easy and Cam had immediately settled her and Eva Marie on the couch with him. Gert and Sally Ann had arrived and were visiting in the kitchen with Aunt

Trudy, Violet, and Karla. Cam's sisters and all of his and her sisters-in-law had Maisy surrounded as they asked her about her cooking show experience

It didn't take but a moment before Vance and Drake moved in for their baby time.

"This is the most beautiful baby in the world," Vance said, smiling like a proud uncle as he carefully took Eva Marie into his arms.

Lana's heart was so full it threatened to explode with happiness as she watched her little big brother cuddle his new niece in his strong arms.

"See, little brother," Drake said, smiling as he also looked at her baby as if he were in love. "That big gold belt buckle you're wearing makes a good elbow rest while you rock our sweet girl."

"Hey that's a good use for it," Vance laughed. And turned so that Libby and Maisy could get a better look at the baby.

Contentment filled Lana as she turned her head to look at Cam. He drew her closer into his side and grinned as she snuggled into him.

"It was hard keeping those two in Las Vegas but

they stayed for you. Vance has barely joined into any conversation about winning the championship. All he's wanted to talk about is Eva Marie." He kissed her ear. "How are you? Do you need anything?"

Lana had been on such an emotional roller coaster for months. Now, she leaned her head against Cam's jaw and tugged on his hand, pulling his arm snug around her as she leaned into him and kissed his hand. "I have everything I could ever need right here in this room with me." He kissed her hair and she closed her eyes…she was in heaven and as she listened to her family all ooh and awe over her sweet baby she felt her mother beside her. Tears pricked her face, and her heart cracked. She turned to Cam. "Ever since I've held Eva Marie in my arms I've felt my mom near, as if I'm holding Eva Marie for both of us. And for the first time ever, I know she's here with me."

"You know she's been with you the whole time. You were just afraid."

She sniffed softly and nodded. "I know. But, I'm not afraid anymore. Thanks for being there for me through all my ups and my downs."

He looked into her eyes and his handsome expression was full of love. "We got married in Las Vegas." Congratulations erupted and then disbelief that Drake would do something so out of character for him. He laughed and Maisy did too.

Libby and Vance grinned from where they stood a few feet away. "Startled us too," Vance said. "But we were proud to witness the midnight wedding."

"*Midnight*." Lana laughed in more disbelief.

"Yes." Maisy chuckled and then turned serious and turned in Drake's arms as she looked up at her husband and met his kiss as he dropped his lips to hers briefly before going on to explain to the silent room of smiling, stunned family. It was just so out of character for completely responsible Drake.

He looked at Lana. "The night you were admitted to the hospital and Cam called to tell us and then told us we should stay in Vegas until Vance competed in the final event two nights away. Well, I knew how worried Cam was and Mom's death weighed heavy on me. And I asked Maisy if she'd marry me right then and there at a Chapel."

"And I said yes. We got married the night I won the contest after Vance finished his next to the last ride and won that."

"I couldn't stand another moment without Maisy being my wife and now she is. We're going to pick out her wedding ring today." He smiled and kissed her again.

Everyone had been stunned and now broke into movement and more congratulations as they moved toward the couple to hug them.

"I'm proud of you," Marcus said shaking his son's hand then clapping him on the shoulder. "Really happy, son."

Lana sighed. "Me too. I think it's romantic and lovely. And I'm so happy for you both."

"Thanks," Drake said, and looked so happy.

As her family and Cam's family continued their hugs and congratulations to both Shar and Gage and Drake and Maisy, she looked at Cam. "I'm so very happy. Are we really going to move to Ransom Creek?"

Cam winked at her. "I'm about to bust I'm so

happy. And yes, I've already called the real estate agent. "Eva Marie needs family around her. And so do we. When all these babies start showing up we're going to be on the road half the time trying to keep up with all of them. Moving to Ransom Creek will at least put us closer to half of them making it easier to spend some time there and some time here in Windswept Bay."

"Wonderful," Lana said. "It just sounds wonderful."

He leaned his forehead to hers and laughed. "It's going to be a wonderful life, Darlin'."

"Oh Cam, it already is," she sighed and knew it was true. So very, wonderfully true.

"Yes, it is," Cam said looking down at their beautiful baby girl and then at her.

And Lana counted her blessings and lifted her lips to his.

Excerpt from

HER COWBOY HERO

Cowboys of Ransom Creek, Book One

CHAPTER ONE

"The horses and the trailer are gone."

What? Lori Calhoun stared at Trip Jensen, her foreman at the Calhoun Ranch and also her partner in the rough stock rodeo contracting business—thanks to her father.

The pit of her stomach knotted as she saw the solemn look in Trip's eyes.

"All five of them?" she asked, fighting the shock of finding out their prized saddle broncs had been stolen.

Trip shifted his weight from one boot to the other. His handsome features twisted with disgust and fury as he squinted at her from beneath the straw Stetson shading his light blue eyes. "Yep. They're gone. But we will find them. Harvey and Mike said they loaded the horses on the trailer before they connected it to the truck. Don't ask me why they did that. Then they went to get the truck—which was for some reason still on the other side of the arena. When they got back the trailer loaded with our horses had disappeared."

She blinked through frustrations strangling her. "That doesn't even sound right. What was Harvey thinking?"

"I don't know," Trip bit out, showing his frustration. "I have no reason to believe that he or Mike had anything to do with the theft—other than lack of good judgement, but believe me, I'm looking into it."

Her stomach churned. Those were her champion rodeo Broncs and the mainstay of the rough stock business. Those horses were heading to the Western

Rodeo Circuit Finals if they kept preforming like they were this year. They were the cornerstone of the business but she didn't need to tell Trip that. Like her, he had a stake in this business and understood all too well how important it was for their horses to be in the finals this year. So much had happened this year, her father had died in a tragic horse accident which that alone still held her in the grips of grief. But on top of that, everyone would be watching to see if she and Trip could continue with the tradition of Calhoun stock in the WRC finals that had begun from the first year her daddy had formed the stock contracting business. Trip had bought half the company only three months before Ray Calhoun's horse threw him and he hit his head and died and left her to take the reins of the ranch and the other half of the stock company. And Lori was struggling.

Add to that her mounting frustration at being forced, by her dad, to work with Trip.

Those frustrations had been mounting for the last five months, threatening to explode and now this…she swung around to stare out the window. Fighting anger and insecurities she slammed her fists to her hips and studied the barns and arenas across the wide yard and gravel parking area. This was the ranch her daddy had built. The ranch that now rested on her shoulders and she felt in every way that she was not living up to expectations.

"Daddy would've been furious right now," she said.

He'd been dead only five months and she felt like she was in over her head. He would be rolling over his grave right now if he knew that on her watch she'd lost such a legacy.

"It's not your fault, Lori. It's not mine either. Someone did this and we're going to find out who. It's that simple. Your dad wouldn't be mad at you. Them— yes. No doubt about that."

She spun back to glare at Trip. "This happened on my watch—and so did that trailer load of steers that someone just drove off the property with last week."

"Lori Lyn Calhoun I'm warning you to stop blaming yourself. You didn't lose those broncs or that load of steers. It's only a matter of time before we catch them. Those rangers will get a lead on them. As for the load of horses, Harvey and Mike lost them on my watch. And I plan to find them."

"Our watch," she snapped, stubbornly. "Do you think Harvey and Mike are guilty?"

"Of carelessness. But until I get better answers as to why they loaded that trailer and then left it unattended with our prized stock in it, I'm not going to be easy to live with. And they won't be careless like that again."

She took a deep breath and tried to hold onto her show of strength but the façade was growing thin. Since her dad's death she felt so alone. Her mother had turned her back on her when she was a baby and it had just been her and her dad. And then, there was Trip…she pushed away the overpowering wish to feel his strong arms around her. Once things had been so easy between them. Once that would have been an option.

But it hadn't been for a very long time. "So, what do we do now?" she asked instead of gaining strength from him.

"I've called the cops and reported it. I've also called the Knight Investigation Agency—since they know the rodeo and investigate incidents for the WRC they may be able to find out more than the police, who basically asked Harvey and Mike a couple of questions and said they'd be in touch if they hear anything. Since this was a WRC sanctioned rodeo the Knights have taken the lead."

"That's good to know. I've met all three brothers, Jesse, Sean and Michael. They're great. And their dad and mine competed against each other in their younger years in the rodeo."

"I think they'll get to the bottom of it."

She bit her lip. "This will be a first that the Calhoun Ranch or the stock company has ever been in the middle of a rodeo investigation."

She didn't think that was a fluke. No, her dad, Ray Calhoun, had been one tough cowboy. He'd built this ranch and the rough stock business from the ground up and he was as tough as the bucking horses they bred. Her daddy was a hard businessman, a hard rider and a harder man when it came to being crossed.

"There's a first for everything," Trip said. "But that doesn't mean we have to like it or take it."

"Right," she grunted. "I'm pretty certain nobody messed with Daddy simply because of who he was." But she wasn't her daddy. She was just his daughter trying hard to step into his boots and knowing no one could ever replace him. She fought off the sudden need to cry and wished she still had her back to Trip.

"You're doing a good job, Lori," he said and took a step toward her but stopped. "Your dad would be proud of you for sticking around and stepping in for him."

For a brief moment it felt like it once had, when things were easy between them…before everything had gotten so complicated.

She sighed. "I'm trying. But this isn't helping." She wanted desperately to live up to the expectation of her dad…her daddy. He deserved only the best she could give because that was what he'd always given to her.

When Lori was two her mother ran off with

another man and hadn't wanted anything to do with Lori or her dad. He had tried to love her enough for himself and her runaway mother and that had meant he'd spoiled her in many ways but he'd raised her to be independent too. And when eventually she'd chosen to take a job in Houston instead of staying here and running the ranch with him, he'd given her his blessing. She'd been in Houston when she'd gotten the call that he was dead.

Devastated had been too small a word for what she'd felt. What she still felt.

She still carried the wound that she'd not been here on the ranch where she belonged when he'd had his accident. She didn't think she would ever get over that.

And now this.

She focused on Trip, standing solid and strong as he waited for her to speak. For only a moment she wished again that she could rest her head on his shoulder and feel the support of his arms around her…but she pushed that thought out of her mind. This was not the time for regrets or a show of weakness. Instead, she pushed her shoulders back and yanked her big girl pants up tight—she was Ray Calhoun's daughter. "What did the Knights say? Fill me in and let's get on this. I do not plan to stand by and let vultures start pecking off bits and pieces of my daddy's legacy."

Trip smiled. "Well, hello, Lori Calhoun. Where the dickens have you been lately?"

Her heart clenched. "Having a pity party. And I just realized my daddy raised me better than that."

She thought she saw approval in Trip's gaze. "The police said they'll call if they hear anything. They're on the lookout for the trailer, though I'm not holding out any hope since whoever did this probably changed the plates. If not, then I figure the trailer will be found abandoned somewhere empty. As for the Knights, Sean Knight was at the rodeo in case a veterinarian was needed since that's his job. He'd already left the grounds but is hanging around the area and not flying home since the next WRC rodeo is in Fort Worth at the

Stockyards next week. So he's supposed to meet me at the arena in Mesquite at three."

"Great. I'll join you, then," she said, glancing at her watch. "When are we leaving?"

"It's a two hour drive from Ransom Springs to the arena so how about right after lunch?"

"Perfect. I'll meet you at the truck at one."

"Sounds good. I better go to my office and get a few things done," he said, then without another word headed out the door of her daddy's office. Her office.

Unable to stop herself she moved to the window and watched him move with purposeful strides across the yard toward the stables that also housed the ranch manager's office—his office.

A decade old longing seeped over her. Their relationship was complicated. And she'd learned to live with things the way they were years ago after he'd headed off to college and left her behind. Thought she might one day get over him…

And then her daddy had hired him on as manager and gone into business with him.

And then he'd complicated things more by dying and leaving her here to sort things out.

Complicated…her life in a nutshell.

It took everything Trip had in him to walk out of that house without pulling Lori into his arms and try to comfort her. She was being too hard on herself, having lost her dad and then stepping into the ownership of the ranch and the rodeo stock company. She had a lot on her shoulders and trying to live up to the expectations of her father or others expectations was not making things any easier. And then dealing with him as ranch manager…things had been strained between them ever since she'd come home from Houston to deal with the ranch's needs after Ray's death.

She had a life in Houston and he wasn't certain if she planned to go back to that life when things were sorted out here or if she planned to stay.

One thing he knew, his time was running out to bridge this canyon between them. And the horses being stolen wasn't helping anything. It was just adding more burden on her already loaded down shoulders.

He hurt for her…it was hard knowing his being here was adding more strain on her. At least he thought it was. It was hard on him. But he was determined to somehow make things right between them.

More Books by Debra Clopton

Turner Creek Ranch Series
Treasure Me, Cowboy (Book 1)
Rescue Me, Cowboy (Book 2)
Complete Me, Cowboy (Book 3)
Sweet Talk Me, Cowboy (Book 4)

New Horizon Ranch Series
Her Texas Cowboy (Book 1)
Rafe (Book 2)
Chase (Book 3)
Ty (Book 4)
Dalton (Book 5)
Treb (Book 6)
Maddie's Secret Baby (Book 7)
Austin (Book 8)

Cowboys of Ransom Creek
Her Cowboy Hero (Book 1)
Bride for Hire (Book 2)
Cooper (Book 3)
Shane (Book 4)
Vance (Book 5)
Drake (Book 6)
Brice (Book 7)

Texas Matchmaker Series

Dream With Me, Cowboy (Book 1)
Be My Love, Cowboy (Book 2)
This Heart's Yours, Cowboy (Book 3)
Hold Me, Cowboy (Book 4)
Be Mine, Cowboy (Book 5)
Marry Me, Cowboy (Book 6)
Cherish Me, Cowboy (Book 7)
Surprise Me, Cowboy (Book 8)
Serenade Me, Cowboy (Book 9)
Return To Me, Cowboy (Book 10)
Love Me, Cowboy (Book 11)
Ride With Me, Cowboy (Book 12)
Dance With Me, Cowboy (Book 13)

Windswept Bay Series

From This Moment On (Book 1)
Somewhere With You (Book 2)
With This Kiss (Book 3)
Forever and For Always (Book 4)
Holding Out For Love (Book 5)
With This Ring (Book 6)
With This Promise (Book 7)
With This Pledge (Book 8)
With This Wish (Book 9)
With This Forever (Book 10)
With This Vow (Book 11)

About the Author

Bestselling author Debra Clopton has sold over 2.5 million books. Her book OPERATION: MARRIED BY CHRISTMAS has been optioned for an ABC Family Movie. Debra is known for her contemporary, western romances, Texas cowboys and feisty heroines. Sweet romance and humor are always intertwined to make readers smile. A sixth generation Texan she lives with her husband on a ranch deep in the heart of Texas. She loves being contacted by readers.

Visit Debra's website at www.debraclopton.com

Sign up for Debra's newsletter at
www.debraclopton.com/contest/

Check out her Facebook at
www.facebook.com/debra.clopton.5

Follow her on Twitter at @debraclopton

Contact her at debraclopton@ymail.com

If you enjoyed reading *With This Vow* I would appreciate it if you would help others enjoy this book, too.

Recommend it. Please help other readers find this book by recommending it to friends, reader's groups and discussion boards.

Review it. Please tell other readers why you liked this book by reviewing it on the retail site you purchased it from or Goodreads. If you do write a review, please send an email to debraclopton@ymail.com so I can thank you with a personal email. Or visit me at: www.debraclopton.com.

www.ingramcontent.com/pod-product-compliance
Lightning Source LLC
Chambersburg PA
CBHW071156180726
48291CB00007B/2475